DEAD BOYS' CLUB

Also by Geoffrey Malone

Brunner

Torn Ear

Kimba

Crocodile River

Elephant Ben

Wolf!

Cadoc

Tiger!

Pirates

DEAD BOYS' CLUB

GEOFFREY MALONE

Hodder
Children's
Books

A division of Hachette Children's Books

Copyright 2013 Geoffrey Malone

First published in Great Britain in 2013
by Hodder Children's Books

The right of Geoffrey Malone to be identified as the Author
of the Work has been asserted by him in accordance with
the Copyright, Designs and Patents Act 1988.

1

A Catalogue record for this book is available from the British Library

ISBN 978 0 340 99960 8

Typeset in Garamond by Avon DataSet Ltd, Bidford-on-Avon, Warwickshire

Printed and bound by CPI Group (UK) Ltd, Croydon, CR0 4YY

The paper and board used in this paperback by Hodder Children's Books
are natural recyclable products made from wood grown in sustainable forests.
The Manufacturing processes conform to the environmental regulations
of the country of origin.

Hodder Children's Books
a division of Hachette Children's Books
338 Euston Road, London NW1 3BH
An Hachette UK company
www.hachette.co.uk

To Claude et Michele Valentin
et toute leur Famille

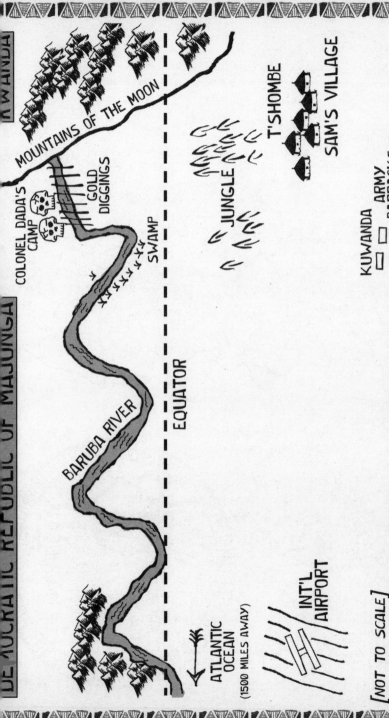

THE MAJUNGA HERALD

Established 1934

'Peace and Prosperity to our Nation.'

GOD'S FREEDOM ARMY SACKS VILLAGE

Eastern Province – Reports are coming in of an attack two days ago on a remote village near the border with Rwanda by the God's Freedom Army faction of rebels. The dissidents, many of whom were reported as being children under the age of twelve, attacked the village of Tshombe last Tuesday, July 23.

Francis Mlindi, 62, the village headman, described what happened as, 'Terrifying'.

'They came out of nowhere,' he said. 'Children firing guns. Killing people and destroying our livestock. Then they took away our young people, boys and girls, and set fire to the village.'

Mr Mlindi was himself brutally assaulted and had a hand cut off by the rebels. He spoke to us from his bed in the regional hospital and pleaded for greater protection from the Army.

Minister of the Interior, Patrick Mumba, told the *Herald* that Majungan Army units were tracking the rebels and would soon bring them to justice. 'There is no place in our country for cut-throats like this,' he added.

The God's Freedom Army faction is led by the self-styled 'Colonel' Dada, a former priest who claims to be guided by religious visions. In previous years, Dada has turned parts of Uganda and Rwanda into a war zone. However, he has recently stepped up his attacks inside our own Eastern Province. This latest outrage will be of the greatest concern to all our citizens.

The *Herald* calls upon the government to take strong and immediate action.

CHAPTER 1

Something was wrong. Sam's eyes flicked open. He was not alarmed – just curious, in a half-awake sort of way. Thirty seconds later he was not so sure. He pushed himself up on his elbows. Was that people shouting? From a long way off? He put his head to one side and listened intently. Nothing more. The sound of his mother and sisters' breathing filled the hut with familiar intensity. Dawn was coming. Thin strips of grey light were starting to show between the slats of the bamboo blind that screened the entrance to the hut. Sam listened to the faint slap-slap they made in the early morning breeze.

His father had fitted the blind only last week, at the end of his army leave. Sam had helped him. Together, they had nailed two pulleys on either side of the doorway, run ropes under the blind and then back up again. And hey presto, it worked. Well, it did after a fashion. Despite their best efforts, it still sagged to one side. His mother had been less impressed. She did not say anything at the time, but her shrug said a lot.

The light was strengthening. In an hour's time, the sun would scorch down and the outside air would shimmer and distort. Now though, it felt cold and the boy shivered. The warmth of the bed rose around his neck and shoulders, tempting him. Gratefully, he snuggled back under his blanket.

His mother mumbled something but he did not catch what she was saying. He held his breath, willing her not to wake up. Obligingly, she drifted back to sleep. Sam was more than happy to lie in bed for a little while longer. All too soon it would be time to get up and begin the day. His sisters would bring back water from the village pump while he got the fire going. That was his job. His mother did the cooking and made the strong, red-coloured tea they always had for breakfast. Then in the afternoon, he would walk out into the surrounding bush and gather the wood they would need for the evening.

A dog barked. It sounded very close. Sam heard both surprise and uncertainty in its growl. The dog must be right outside. Its growling grew louder and more threatening. Sam sat up. He was right. Something was different this morning. Where were all the cockerels? None of them were crowing. Every family in the village had a rooster and half a dozen hens as well. Normally they would be making enough noise to wake the dead. So why were they being so quiet today?

He pushed his blanket back and padded across the floor. One of his sisters was awake and called after him. He pushed past the blind and stood, bleary-eyed, outside the hut. It was full dawn and the land was flooded with brilliant light. Across the river on the far side of the village, a range of low hills flared into glowing bands of orange, red and purple rock.

A family of goats was feeding on a nearby patch of grass. Otherwise, no one else was about. He was glad to see the fire had kept going overnight. There was a dull glow deep inside the heap of wood ash. He stooped to pick up a handful of sticks and drop them on top of the glowing embers. He yawned and scratched his bottom.

The dog growled again. It was standing just metres from the hut. It stood motionless, its tail held rigid. He picked up a pebble and threw it at the animal. The dog ignored him and started to snarl. It was really angry about something. He found a large stick and hurried over to see what was bothering it. It could be a jackal, but it was much more likely to be a snake. He came up behind the dog, scolding it in a low voice with a hand held carefully in front of his eyes. It might be a spitting cobra. There were a lot of them about.

He stopped abruptly, his mouth opening in disbelief. There were boys running towards him. His own age. Armed with rifles. Wearing some sort of uniform. Fifty metres away. A long line of them, racing towards his village. There were men too. Four or five of them. With machine guns. Coming out of the low scrub not far behind. Urging them on.

Sam yelled at the top of his voice. The dog bounded forward, barking hysterically. There was a burst of gunfire and bullets thudded into the ground. He saw sand kicking up in front of him. Panic stricken, he turned and ran.

He knew who they were. Rebels! Killers! Every one of them. Crazed children, high on drugs, scared of nothing and nobody. 'If they ever come here,' his father had warned, 'drop everything. Just run and hide!'

And now they were here! God's Freedom Army, or whatever their name was. 'Bringers of blood and suffering.' That's how Father Benoit had described them.

There was more firing now over on the other side of the village. Bursts of gunfire that sounded like swarms of angry hornets. More bullets ripped over Sam's head and tore into the sides of huts. People were swarming out into the open, shouting and confused. Sam skidded to a halt beside his own hut and saw his mother standing in the doorway, staring wide-eyed at him.

She was shouting. He saw her mouth moving but couldn't hear. He grabbed her by the arm. 'Run!' he screamed. 'It's the rebels! They're coming! Get away!' A man barged into him. Sam slipped and fell. There were others close behind him. He flung himself to one side and rolled out of their way. Close by, a child was screaming. A horrible, animal shriek that went on and on. Sam scrambled to his feet, coughing as a cloud of dust enveloped him.

Somehow he got clear and began searching for his mother. He tried to fight his way back towards the hut but the crowd was too dense and carried him along with it. He saw faces he knew all around him. Terrified faces that kept coming and going. There was more firing. It was everywhere. The crowd stumbled and hesitated and backed away like a herd of uncertain cattle. He had a sudden glimpse of one of the rebels. A boy like himself, not much more than twelve, firing a gun into the air. He was grinning. Broadly.

The sight of that boy soldier decided Sam. They were not going to catch him. He must get away. Fast! There were places he knew out in the bush where he could hide until this horror was over. Only God knew where his mother and sisters were. And he must find them.

He forced his way through the melee – ducking, side-stepping and fighting to get by. Voices rose in a wild hubbub all around him. There was more shooting. Where did they get all the ammunition from? Were they shooting people or just firing into the air? The crowd had come to a clumsy halt so Sam guessed the rebels had them surrounded. Terror seized him. Had he left it too late? He thrust past a pregnant woman, cursing her protests. She must get out of his way. Why couldn't she see that? He had to get away. There was thick bush beyond the village and clumps of trees and patches of head-high elephant grass. Perfect hiding.

He staggered out into the open and was shocked to see a rebel right in front of him. One of the adults. He was in full combat kit with a spare bandolier of ammunition draped across his chest. He was looking the other way and yelling at someone. Sam did not hesitate. He put his head down and ran. There was movement at the corner of his eye. He looked and saw a group of boy soldiers pointing at him. He heard them shout. There was a single shot then a fusillade. He heard the bullets zip past. Then he was racing towards the line of scrub.

There were more yells and another ragged volley. Sam ran with bursting lungs, knowing they must be following him. If they caught him . . . He thrust that thought to the back of his mind. Seconds later, he snatched a look back. They were still there. Six of them at least. Maybe more. The ground in front of him was broken and littered with rocks and patches of loose shale. One false step and he'd be down with a twisted ankle.

As he ran, Sam felt a cold dread rising inside him. He hadn't made a clean break and now they were after him. Boy soldiers, much fitter than he was and no more than sixty or seventy metres away. He stared in front of him then looked around wildly. He didn't recognize anything. There were no familiar trees or rocks. Nothing he could remember. His mind had gone blank. He was lost! But how could he be? All those hiding places. Where were they? Vanished like the early morning mist. He was running for his life with a pack of predators at his heels and no idea where he was going. He sobbed. He couldn't help it.

He made himself snatch another look behind. There they were. Bobbing shapes, following him with the determination of a pack of hyenas. 'When hyenas find a really old lion, they follow it for weeks until the lion is too weak to fight. Then they move in and kill it,' his father had told him. 'Hyenas never give up. They're like those Canadian Mounties. They always get their man!' He had laughed and slapped his thigh at the joke.

Was that only last week? It seemed a hundred years ago. And at that moment, he saw the bush. It was not really a bush. More a huge tangle of undergrowth that over the years had spread and wrapped itself around a clump of thorn trees. It took up most of the shallow ravine below him. Without hesitation, Sam ran towards it, dodging between a dozen or more towering anthills. They would screen him. The slope was steeper than he expected and he raced out of control down the side of the valley. He ran around the bush, searching for somewhere to get in. After an eternity, he found it.

With a prayer there would not be a puff adder sleeping there, Sam closed his eyes and burrowed inside. He could feel thorns slashing at his face and arms and ripping his red T-shirt. There was no feeling of pain. That would come later. As soon as he was in cover, he stopped to listen. Silence. He laid his forehead on the ground and listened to the pounding of his heart. And waited . . .

CHAPTER 2

He had no idea how long he lay there. It seemed an eternity. He began to say his prayers and found himself promising God that he'd be better behaved in the future. If God would only help him now . . . The silence continued. A bird began to sing from somewhere overhead. He listened to it with a sense of growing confidence. The rebels must be miles away. He had outwitted them. Sam grinned and slapped a hand on the ground in triumph.

So when he heard their shouts, he listened in sheer disbelief. Their calls were faint at first but grew steadily louder. There was no mistake. They were coming towards him. Running. They sounded angry. Very angry. There was a sudden loud yell, close to his hiding place. Sam panicked, bit his tongue and lay rigid. More shouts. Then someone gave a whoop and Sam's heart stopped.

With a sinking feeling, he wondered how good their bush craft was. Would they spot the scuff marks he must have left, squeezing inside the undergrowth? Or the bruised leaves and broken twigs at the entrance?

He heard a loud click and flinched as a gun fired a long burst. Bullets sprayed randomly all around him. One of them clipped a branch above his head. A splinter of wood landed on the back of his hand. Sam stared at it in horror. Another burst of gunfire. Then the bitter smell of cordite. And silence. The rebels were listening.

Sam began to tremble. His whole body shook. There was nothing he could do to stop it. Could they hear him? He clenched his teeth to stop them clicking. And waited. Were they expecting him to make the next move? How could they be so sure that he was in here? Sam thrust his body even harder into the ground. Minutes passed, and with them came a terrible feeling that he was being watched. He fought the compulsion to look for as long as he could. But eventually, and with great care, he turned his head a centimetre at a time and peered up through the thorns, to the dappled sunshine beyond.

A face was looking back at him. A face with two

black, unwinking eyes. Eyes that peered in at him. There was a yell of triumph and the sound of running feet. The next moment, the bush began to shake. Broad-bladed machetes slashed down through the branches towards him. Triumphant hands snatched at his body. He curled up in a ball and tried to shrink back into the earth. A cudgel thumped into his ribs. In the end, he let them drag him out.

There were eight of them and a smaller child who looked about six years old. The assault rifle he carried was almost as tall as he was. They stood around Sam, assessing him with dispassionate interest. They might have been looking at a dog or a dead bullock. The leader jabbed him hard in the stomach with the muzzle of his gun. Sam gasped in pain and, without thinking, knocked it away. The rebel sprang back and thrust the rifle into his face. They stared at each other, both of them furious. Sam heard someone else shout and the rebels started to laugh. The small boy kicked him on the leg and pointed at the growing wet patch on the front of his shorts. Sam looked down and felt ashamed.

They marched him back to the village with his hands on top of his head. It did not take long. The rebels had herded the villagers into the open space between the huts. A dozen boy soldiers formed a circle, menacing them with their guns. The village men stood with their arms folded, staring at the ground. The women huddled together. Most of them were crying. Every now and then one of them would make a frightened little dart to drag a small child back to their side. No one spoke.

A rifle butt hit Sam between the shoulder blades and he pitched forward into the crowd. His sisters appeared and helped pull him to his feet. He caught a glimpse of his mother then lost her in the crush of faces.

When he got his breath back, he stood on tiptoe and looked around. Some of the rebels were going from hut to hut, pulling out sacks of maize, tins of cooking oil and whatever else caught their fancy. They piled them up in a heap in the open. He also saw two dead bodies. An old woman lay sprawled at the entrance to her hut. She still held a wooden club in an outstretched hand. The front of her dress was black with blood.

The other corpse made him cry out in disbelief. It was Paul, the village carpenter. He lay on his back with his arms flung wide. He was naked except for a pair of green underpants. Tears ran down Sam's face. Paul was a friend of his father's. They played dominoes together most nights, when the corporal was home on leave. Now, Paul lay in the dust with a long red gash down one side of his chest. A goat was sniffing at his head.

The rebels were assembling in front of the crowd. Sam counted five grown men and at least twenty boys. One of the men fired into the air and the villagers became very still.

A large, heavily-muscled man walked slowly forward and stood facing the villagers. The sun glinted on his wrap-around dark glasses. He wore a full necklace of lion claws around his neck. Sam shivered. He had never seen anyone so full of menace before.

The man put his hands on his hips and shouted.

'You people are in trouble. You are my enemy. Everyone in this village is my enemy. You give succour and help to the army of Majunga. But not to us. Not to those who fight to bring you a better life. You do not support God's Freedom Army!'

He stopped and looked around. The village women were starting to moan. They had all heard the stories. A man standing in front of Sam rocked back and forth on his heels. His breath came out in a loud hiss.

The rebel leader was shouting again. 'Do you know who I am?' He thrust his chin at the crowd and scowled. 'I am the man who frightens your women and little children late at night.'

Behind him, some of the rebels whooped and laughed.

'I am Captain Simba!' he cried and shook his fists at the crowd.

The woman beside Sam began to wail. The men glanced at each other and quickly looked away. There was no one in eastern Majunga who had not heard of Simba or his band of killers. The Majungan army had been chasing them for months.

'Who is your headman?' Captain Simba shouted. 'Where is the man who dares to defy me? Bring him to me!'

The villagers shrank aside to reveal the headman. They looked from him to Captain Simba and back again. *They don't mean to act like cowards*, Sam thought, *that's just how life goes*. There was a pause while the stooping figure came slowly out. He was grey and old and wise. His name was Francis Mlindi. Sam stared as the old man put his shoulders back and struggled to stand erect. *He's showing he's not afraid*, Sam considered, as he watched him shuffle forward.

He remembered an American film called *Dead Man Walking*. It had been shown on national television a couple of weeks ago. The whole village had squeezed into the schoolhouse to watch it.

Is this going to be the same? he wondered. Were they

all really inside some huge film set? And would he wake up from this nightmare, any moment now? Sam looked down at the slashes and cuts to his own arms and chest and knew this was no dream.

There was a tree stump in the middle of the village. Captain Simba strode over and stood beside it. Slowly, the headman approached. Simba beckoned him to hurry.

The villagers fell silent as the headman stood before Simba.

'Kneel!' the rebel ordered. 'Put your right hand here where I can hold it.'

The headman did as he was told. Captain Simba grasped his hand.

'Why are they shaking hands?' a man beside Sam whispered. 'What does it mean?'

Simba looked around at the boy soldiers. 'Dinka!' he called. 'Come here!'

The boy who had pointed the rifle in Sam's face ran over. He laid his AK-47 on the ground and tugged at something behind his back. A blade flashed in the sunlight. He held it high over his head. The next moment it came down with a thud and severed Mlindi's hand at the wrist. The headman doubled up over the tree stump, too shocked to cry out.

Captain Simba laughed and picked up the hand.

He held it by the fingers and showed it to them. He pretended to throw the hand into the crowd and laughed again as the villagers shrank back. Then he tossed it at a passing dog.

'This is what will happen to all of you who refuse to cooperate,' he shouted. 'You must do as I say.'

Sam glared at the man. He had never hated anyone or anything as much before.

Like everyone else, the boy knew that death had come to their village. And there was nothing he could do about it.

CHAPTER 3

Five thousand kilometres away, in a small town in
Belgium, a man hunched his neck into the folds of a
heavy leather coat. The TV weatherman was right, he
thought. 'Snow by midnight,' he'd said. And Mr
Schratte could smell it coming. The usual February
drizzle was giving way to an icy, slanting rain. In this
part of town, the street lighting was erratic. But he
could still see the growing patches of sleet, sticking to
the cobbles. There could be anything from five to
ten centimetres of snow by morning – but so what?
Mr Schratte was not worried. Belgium was an
efficient country and the roads would soon be
cleared. And in any case, his large Mercedes estate,
parked in the town centre half a kilometre away,
was fitted with snow chains.

This part of town was always quiet. At night, it felt deserted. The streets were narrow and lined with pinched little houses. They looked more like seaside cabins than proper homes. Mr Schratte knew them well; he had grown up in one many years ago. Before Africa. Before his name became one that many people knew. Before a lot of things.

Nothing much seemed to have changed here over the intervening years. Old-fashioned wooden poles still carried the telephone and electricity lines. And the houses were already shuttered tight against the evening cold.

It was a place the police rarely came to. But if they did, they came in strength. People here knew when to look the other way. Their lives had been a struggle since birth and would always be so. 'Keep your nose out of other people's business. You've got enough troubles of your own' was their attitude. This was why he had suggested meeting here, at the bar, when Jean Morrell had called him out of the blue, twenty-four hours ago.

He sneezed and wiped his nose on the back of his glove. Jean was a good boy. No! Hardly a 'boy' now, he corrected himself. Jean Morrell was the youngest son of his best friend from the Majungan days. Mr Schratte smiled at the memory. *Long time ago*, he thought. When the Cold War between Communist Russia and the West was the only game in town. And Majunga and other African countries like it were the battlefields the great powers fought over.

Not that *they* ever got their hands dirty, he reflected. They used mercenaries like himself to do the actual killing and the rest of the business. That was the time when news of 'Black Jack' Schratte and his commando of five hundred ex-soldiers was regularly plastered across the front of the world's newspapers.

Mr Schratte had no regrets. He had done very well out of Africa. There were still fortunes to be made for today's entrepreneurs. But only for those who knew the right people and who were quick to learn where real power lay. Mr Schratte was the friend of presidents and jailers alike. In fact, many police forces kept a file on him. No other European knew Africa as well as he did and he was proud of his knowledge.

For the hundredth time that day, he wondered what Jean Morrell wanted. And why the secrecy? He had not seen or heard from him for over two years. Morrell had wasted no time on pleasantries when he'd telephoned the day before. He was now based in Majunga and was flying to Europe that same evening. He must talk to Schratte as soon as he arrived and no one else was to know.

'Come and have dinner with me,' Mr Schratte had cried enthusiastically. 'Brussels is full of good restaurants.'

'No way!' Morrell had replied. 'I don't want some clever journalist seeing us together and getting nosy. You must know somewhere . . . safe?'

Mr Schratte did. Several. He replayed the conversation in his mind and gave a satisfied grunt. If this was something to do with Majunga, then Morrell was in luck. The country was near the top of his list of good places to do business in. He had known its President, Robert Nyuma, for almost half a lifetime. And Nyuma was a good man to know. A shiver of excitement was gathering between Mr Schratte's shoulder blades. Something big was happening. He knew the signs.

Snowflakes were falling now in heavy swirls. His shoes scrunched noisily. At the next corner, he looked back then turned quickly into a side street. A hundred metres further on, the red neon light of the Amitié Bar shone out like a welcoming beacon. Mr Schratte hurried towards it.

Ahead of him, he noticed a car parked half on the pavement on the other side of the road. He eyed it carefully. No visible tracks behind the rear wheels and the snow settling on the bonnet. So the engine was cold and it had been there for some time. Not the police then, he decided. Just a harmless, civilian car.

The door of the bar was heavy and he had to use his shoulder to push it open. The reinforced panel of glass at head height was pitted and scarred. Conversation faded as he stepped inside. A blast of hot air fogged his glasses. He stamped the snow from his shoes and stepped over the pool of black slush in front of him. The half a dozen young men sitting at the bar turned back to follow the football match on the screen above them.

The barman gave him a nod. He was a powerfully built man with a head covered in blond bristles. He wore a T-shirt at least one size too small. He looked like the 'Mr Muscle' oven-cleaner advert.

'I'm expecting a friend,' Mr Schratte told him.

The man pointed to a table in an alcove. 'I'll see you're not disturbed,' he said, and quietly added, 'Sir.' Mr Schratte sat down and the barman brought him a beer and a packet of peanuts.

A car drew up outside. The bar window was running with moisture. Mr Schratte rubbed at it with the sleeve of his coat and peered out. A taxi. In the yellow glow of its roof light, he watched the rear door open and a man get out. It was impossible to see his features. The man stooped and paid the driver. Then he straightened, looked up at the bar sign and walked to the door. The taxi drove off. *So far so good*, thought Mr Schratte. Plain clothes police would have come in their own vehicle. A different sort of enemy would have kept the cab waiting as a getaway car.

The door swung open and Jean Morrell stood there. Mr Schratte got to his feet and smiled in pleasure. Morrell lifted an arm in salute.

Jean Morrell was a short, stocky man with a head of wavy brown hair. He grinned at Mr Schratte and came over. He walked with a limp these days. The two men embraced and slapped each other on the back.

'It's been a long time, Jean,' Mr Schratte told him.

'Far too long,' the other agreed. 'I thought perhaps you had retired.'

Mr Schratte laughed. 'I might still do. Depends on what you've got for me.'

There was a loud cheer from the men at the bar. On the television, footballers were hugging one another. Morrell looked around the rest of the room and slid a hand inside his jacket. He brought out a small drawstring bag and handed it to Mr Schratte.

'Take a look but don't make a big performance of it. And don't take anything out. Not here,' he warned.

Mr Schratte opened the bag carefully and glanced down at the small pieces of rock inside. He frowned and began to rub them with his fingers. Then he dug his thumbnail into one and studied the result. He stared at Morrell.

'Is this what I think it is?'

The younger man smiled. 'It's top quality. I had them tested this morning when I got in. I'm sitting on top of a gold mine. And I'm the only one who knows where it is. Interested?'

CHAPTER 4

Captain Simba held up an arm and studied the watches on his left wrist. He wore three of them and they flashed in the sun. 'Line them up!' he shouted. 'Men, women and children. C'mon! Hurry!'

A boy soldier raised his AK-47 and fired a long burst over the villagers' heads. Captain Simba grinned as the people milled around in panic. *Just like chickens*, he thought. *When there's a jackal around.*

The older rebels swung their rifle butts and kicked and cursed the villagers into line. 'OK, Boss!' they shouted when they had finished. Captain Simba clapped his hands and everyone looked at him. He stood with both thumbs hooked into his web belt. He rocked back on his heels and examined the rag-tag crowd of villagers in front of him.

All these people, the Captain thought. *Going about their dull little lives. No better than the goats their children herd. And then, one day, I, Captain Simba, come into their lives. And, wham! Shazam! I change everything.* He smiled. This was how God must feel. And God had chosen him to share in this amazing power. Sometimes life was good. Very good indeed.

He slapped the holster strapped to his leg and slowly pulled out a pistol. He pointed the gun at the villagers. 'I want recruits,' he shouted. 'Strong, willing recruits to join me in doing God's work.' He paused and waited, watching the crowd for any reaction. Sometimes the odd individual *did* volunteer. But that was rare. More often than not, the village people would be too frightened to come forward. Or too full of wickedness to take that one, all-important step. A simple act that would save their lives.

No one moved. A woman's crying grew louder. A small child suddenly broke ranks and scuttled away from its mother. A boy soldier ran after it and dragged it back. Captain Simba waited a little while longer, then, with a shake of his head, stalked towards the line of children. Boy soldiers with their AK-47s at the ready formed an escort. Sam felt the man's gaze fall on him.

'That one!' Captain Simba called.

'He's wet himself,' a rebel jeered. 'He's only a baby.'

25

'He ran away!' another one called.

'He's big and he's strong. He'll do,' Simba told them.

Hands grabbed Sam and dragged him to one side. A small rebel pointed his gun at him. 'Stay there!' he shouted. 'And don't move!'

Other village boys were picked out and sent to join him. Then, three girls. They stood like cattle, too frightened and ashamed to even look at each other. Sam stared at the flat-topped acacia trees that surrounded the village and the familiar thatched huts underneath. This was his home. Where he had grown up. His family had always lived here. They had been happy and content. He turned quickly and scanned the line of women, looking for his mother and sisters.

The rebels were pulling some of the women out of line. There was already a small group standing apart. Something told him that he would never see any of them again. A lump formed in his throat. His eyes blurred. He shouted their names.

A rebel screamed something. Sam turned to face him. A rifle caught him hard in the kidneys. He gasped at the pain and for a long moment stood, bent over, fighting for breath. The rebel was coming at him again, gesticulating with his AK-47. Sam saw the black hole of his mouth and knew the boy was shouting at him.

Fury seized him. Who were these people? What gave them the right to do this? For the first time in his life, he felt hate. Pure, devouring hate. There was no pain any more. No fear of the consequences. Just the throbbing of blood in his head and the need to tear this boy apart with his bare hands.

He ran at the rebel and lashed out with his fists. His knuckles caught the boy hard on the side of his head, just above the ear. The boy staggered and went over backwards, dropping his gun in the dust. Sam stood over him, his fists bunched. He reached down to drag the boy to his feet.

The village children were shrieking at the tops of their voices, some cheering him on, others crying in fear, terrified for him and themselves. The rebels were cursing and shouting at one another. Guns were pointing at Sam. Nervous fingers were tightening on triggers. He looked round at them as if in a dream and his feeling of invincibility slowly dissolved. He let go of the rebel, who squirmed away. Sam's head went down and he let his fists drop.

What have I done? he thought.

The boy he had hit came up and crowded him until they stood chest to chest. Sam recognised him. The boy who had chopped off the headman's hand. Dinka. His eyes glittered, snake-like with menace. Sam's stomach heaved and he felt his knees begin to shake.

'You're a dead man,' Dinka hissed, and he spat in Sam's face.

'Break it up! Break it up! I haven't got time for all this!' Captain Simba shouted, thrusting himself between the two boys.

Sam stepped back, only too glad. He turned away and went to join the other village children. They shrank away from him.

Dinka's eyes followed Sam. Meanwhile Captain Simba pushed up the boy's rifle and rubbed his head, playfully.

'You're not to kill him. Do you hear, Dinka?' he warned. 'Not yet anyway. The Colonel wants every last volunteer. You get me?'

Dinka said nothing.

'Right!' Simba shouted and clapped his hands energetically. 'Tie them together in groups of three. Then load 'em up. Time we were out of here!'

A rope was knotted around Sam's waist and pulled tight. A large tin of cooking oil was thrust at him. 'You! Take this!' a rebel ordered.

Obediently, Sam held out his arms and took it. He gasped. It was both heavy and slippery. He almost dropped it.

'Hold it! You drop it and I'll drop you!'

He clutched the drum to him and staggered. How long did they expect him to carry this thing for? He took several deep breaths to calm himself.

Ten minutes later, Sam and a dozen other children left their village. They staggered along in single file, terrified of dropping the sacks of ground nuts or the tins of cooking oil they carried. The rope around their waists jerked and pulled and cut into the soft skin of their stomachs. On either side, the rebels kept pace, menacing them with weapons, urging them on.

Not long after, they heard a sudden, heavy burst of gunfire. It came from behind them. There were screams too, faint but unmistakable. Then, single shots which went on for a long time. Sam sneaked a look back. Above the distant trees, a column of brown smoke climbed up into the morning sky. A rebel saw what he was doing and broke into a stream of curses. He aimed a kick at Sam's leg. Sam flinched and nearly fell. Afterwards, he barely noticed it. His mind was too full of the horror of what must be happening in the village to care.

They marched all day under the immensity of the African sun. At first, the boy soldiers shouted to one another and laughed and cracked jokes. But quite soon, even they fell silent. The children stumbled along like oxen, heads down, their eyes fixed unseeingly on the heels of the person in front. A cloud of flies and other biting insects hung over them, crawled across their faces, went inside their nostrils, fed greedily from the corners of their mouths. For most of the day, their intense buzzing was the only sound Sam heard.

At midday, the terrain began to change. Deep valleys cut across the ground in front of them. For the village children, the nightmare became worse. Still roped together, they stumbled down hillsides, frantically side-stepping the boulders that littered the place. The loads they carried now acted as counter-weights that threatened to throw them off balance. A fall here would bring the others down as well. And if they couldn't get up and continue? Sam had no illusions about what would happen then.

Later, they came to a river. Captain Simba held up a hand and the column came to a ragged halt. Dinka and two other boy soldiers went ahead. For a while the rebels scouted along the riverbank. Sam watched them, not caring whether he lived or died. The flies no longer bothered him. He could cope with them. But his body was another matter. The muscles in his legs and shoulders were on fire. And more than anything in the world, he needed water to drink!

He had no idea how long they waited there. It may

only have been a matter of minutes. Soon enough, they were on the move again and this time Sam became aware of the blisters on his heels and feet. He hobbled along, bent over in a crouch, until the new pain fused with everything else. The people in front of him had to be feeling just as bad and for some reason this gave him a tiny piece of encouragement.

They straggled along beside the river. Sam looked at it longingly. The level was low and, in parts, had all but dried up. There was enough water left in some pools, however, for him to imagine running towards them and leaping in. He indulged in this daydream until he spotted the open snout of a large crocodile lying motionless in the mud, watching him. Looking more carefully, he saw several more.

Eventually, late in the afternoon, they reached the fringe of the rainforest. They stopped just inside the cover of the trees. Captain Simba walked back along the line of the village children.

'We stay here for the night,' he told them. 'Make yourselves at home.'

Most of the children slumped to their knees and rolled over on to the ground. Some of them went to sleep there and then. Sam slowly sat down on top of his drum of oil and began to unlace his shoes. His tortured feet felt better with them off. Both were badly blistered and one of his heels had rubbed raw. There was a lot of blood in that shoe.

His father had given him the trainers as a birthday present. It would be a long time before he wore them again. He tied the laces together and hung them around his neck.

Two boy soldiers appeared. One held up a tin water bottle and showed it to them. Sam stared at it with longing. His throat was so parched it hurt to swallow. Clumsily, he pushed himself up and got to his feet.

'One swig each!' the rebel shouted. 'Any more and he'll shoot you.' He jerked a thumb at his companion. 'Who's first?'

Later that night, it began to rain. A persistent rain that fell in noisy drops. At first they lay there, tortured by the sound. Then they tried catching it in cupped hands. But what little they caught only made their thirst worse. It was pitch black on the floor of the forest and they were still tied together. Soon, fear of what might be lurking amongst the trees drove them to curl up together in a whimpering, frightened huddle.

CHAPTER 5

'Gentlemen,' called Mr Schratte, 'I want you to meet a friend of mine. He's the son of the toughest soldier Belgium has ever produced. And I'd trust him with my life. Let me introduce Mr Jean Morrell.'

There was a polite smattering of applause from the other three men sitting around the mahogany table. They were all expensively dressed. Two of them had heavy gold rings on their fingers. They looked powerful. They had known Schratte for many years and trusted him. The name Morrell was one they also knew but this was the first time any of them had met this particular member of the family. They were curious about him and eager to find out what Schratte was up to.

Mr Schratte put his arm around Morrell's shoulder.

It was a gesture the men understood. Next, he slid a small leather pouch down the table towards them.

'Take a look,' he told them. 'Take a good look. And rejoice!'

He watched their faces and smiled. 'They're genuine. Pure gold. As good a quality as my experts have seen in years.' He turned to Morrell. 'Tell them,' he ordered. 'From the beginning. Just like you told me.'

Jean Morrell licked his lips. 'It's like this,' he began. 'I look after a big chunk of Majunga for the United Nations. I'm in charge of the administration there. Getting things done. Building schools and bridges. Advising international charities on the ground. I talk to the village elders. Pick up local gossip. That sort of thing.'

They stared at him, coldly weighing him up.

'So you're effectively your own boss,' Mr Schratte prompted.

Morrell nodded and reached over the table to pick up the pouch. 'I found these beauties a week ago,' he told them. 'Right in the middle of my area. Pure luck. I was out with my driver, just checking on a couple of things. The dust was bad that day and we were really thirsty. So we parked under some trees by a river, and while my guy was getting the brew on, I went for a look-around.

'We were on top of this huge bank of sand,' he went on, 'with the river at the bottom. I guess it was about ten metres high. Anyway, halfway down or so, I saw a whole lot of little blue butterflies I had never seen before. They're a hobby of mine,' he told them. 'Butterflies, I mean.'

No one said a word.

'There was a big ledge near them, so I slid down to take a look. That's when I discovered this!' He picked up a piece of rock and rolled it in his hand. 'I spent the next couple of minutes digging. You can see what I found.'

One of the men thrust his chair back and cursed fluently in Italian. 'He found gold just like that?' he demanded to the room at large. 'He has the luck of the devil!'

Mr Schratte interrupted. 'I should tell you that Jean here is a qualified mining engineer.'

'How big could this thing be?' A small man with a beard demanded.

Morrell flung out his hands. 'The gold-bearing vein might just be in the spot where I found it. Or else the whole riverbank could be full of the stuff. I don't know. I didn't hang around.'

'So who else knows?' the Italian asked. 'Who else have you told?'

Morrell shook his head. 'No one. Nobody. Only the people in this room.'

'What about your driver?' the third man challenged.

'He didn't see anything,' Morrell insisted. 'And I made a note of where we were on the GPS.'*

'So you're the only person who knows exactly where the gold is?' the bearded man said quietly.

Morrell nodded. 'As I said, I made a note of the coordinates. I can find the place again in a sandstorm if I have to. No problem.'

'Then all we need do,' chipped in the third man, 'is to hold your feet to a fire long enough for you to give us the information.' He laughed, then, seeing Mr Schratte's face said, 'Sorry, Jack. Just joking.'

The bearded man held up a hand. 'Sounds interesting,' he said guardedly. 'Where do we come in?'

'Look, I know it's early days still,' Mr Schratte told them. 'I mean, we haven't even established just how big this find is. But I'm offering you the chance to get in on the ground floor. We need to put up some money in a hurry to get things moving. After that, it should be easy enough.'

The third man shook his head. 'Wait! I can see a

* GPS: Global Positioning System.

whole lot of problems coming up.'

'Like what?' Mr Schratte challenged.

'Like security,' the other replied. 'Once news of this find gets out, every man, woman and child in Majunga will be heading there to get a piece of the action.'

The Italian agreed. 'You'll need a whole army of mercenaries to keep them out. And that'll cost a fortune. Big bucks. Those sort of guys don't come cheap any more.'

The man with the beard drummed his fingers on the table. 'And then there's the politicians to deal with.' He shook his head regretfully. 'Pity,' he said. 'It could have been good. Thanks for letting us know—'

'But it still *is* good!' Mr Schratte interrupted. 'And it's going to be even better. Where's your faith? Has Black Jack Schratte ever let you down? Let my friend Jean here continue.'

Morrell took a deep breath. 'If you don't mind me saying so,' he began, 'you people are way behind the times.'

'You saying we don't know what we're talking about?' The Italian scowled.

'No! No,' Morrell assured him. 'Let me start again.' He thought for a moment. 'You ever heard of child soldiers?'

They all had. 'Vicious little brats!'

Morrell nodded. 'I come across a lot of people in my job,' he continued. 'And the most interesting man I've ever met has just moved his operation into my area. His name is Colonel Dada. "Dada the Merciful", as he likes to call himself.'

'What's so good about him?' demanded the third man.

Morrell laughed. 'Nothing! He's a psychopath. A cold-blooded killer. He dresses like a priest and carries an AK-47 on his shoulder, night and day. He's a warlord. He's got ten adults and anything up to a hundred of these child soldiers under his command. They're all armed to the teeth and as dangerous as a pack of wild dogs. But here's the good part.'

'*Good* part?' asked the Italian, waving a cigar at Morrell. 'What good part?'

'These children. They worship him,' Morrell told them. 'Dada's like a father and a mother to them. He's also their leader. He's got life and death over them. They all believe they've been hand-picked to become members of "God's Freedom Army". That's what he calls this rabble. But to them, he *is* God. They obey him like dogs. I've seen them.'

The men stared at Morrell, puzzled. 'So?' one of them asked.

Morrell's voice rose in excitement. 'So, Dada tells

me he's been running a gold mining operation in the Congo for the past six months. Up near the Rwandan border.'

'Why did he quit?' the bearded man asked.

'The government there did the dirty and hired a bigger outfit to take over the gold diggings. The Colonel's boys were outgunned. It happens.'

The third man shrugged. 'That's all very sad for this Colonel Dada guy. So what do you want us to do about it?'

Mr Schratte put a hand on Morrell's arm. 'My turn. OK.' Schratte studied them carefully. 'This is what happens. Morrell flies to Majunga tonight. He goes back to the river on his own and does a proper search. If he finds nothing worthwhile, we forget all about this meeting. End of story. But, if he strikes lucky, I want you all to come in with me.'

In the silence that followed, they listened to the wail of a police car speeding down the road outside.

'Morrell has done some talking with Colonel Dada. Just in general terms, to see if he'd be interested. He is. This is the deal, so far.' Mr Schratte licked his lips, nervously. 'For a cash payment of fifty thousand US dollars down, Colonel Dada will set up the gold diggings, sell permits, shovels and other equipment to the miners, administer the entire operation and hand over fifty per cent of the turnover to us, each and every month. I'll be putting in two of my own trusted men to work with his middlemen. To make sure everything is straight.'

'That's a lot of money for Dada,' someone said quietly.

'And a lot of money for us,' Mr Schratte said.

'What about the politicians?' the Italian asked. 'What's their part in all this?'

'The President of Majunga is an old friend of mine,' Mr Schratte told them. 'I can't say any more about that until we get Morrell's final report from the river. But if it's positive, we'll be able to work something out.'

'You're forgetting the security,' the Italian asked. 'The place will be heaving with people wanting to dig. Who's gonna control that lot?'

Morrell answered. 'The child soldiers. That's their job. They work for peanuts and they'll do whatever Dada tells them to. They'll make sure the miners don't steal any gold.'

'How are they going to stop them?' the Italian wanted to know. 'They're kids.'

Morrell smiled to himself and shook his head. 'They'll shoot 'em dead. Then and there. Colonel Dada's orders.'

Mr Schratte flung his arms wide. 'It's a gamble,' he exclaimed. 'What isn't? But I've known many worse. I invite you all to back us. I don't think you'll regret it!'

CHAPTER 6

Sam woke in panic. He was drowning! Water was flooding into his nostrils and filling the back of his mouth. He tried to swallow but there was too much of it. It was all over his face. He fought for breath and struggled to get up. Something was holding him back. He got as far as his knees and the water stopped. He was aware then of the rope around his waist and people on either side. Children like himself.

He could see them clearly. It was almost daylight. What were they all doing out here in the open, roped together like oxen? He heard laughter behind him and turned to see Dinka and a much smaller rebel standing there, grinning.

Dinka held up a water bottle and shook it. The water sloshed inside. Sam's father carried a similar bottle clipped to his web belt. Casually, Dinka tilted the bottle, and they all watched the water form a small puddle on the forest floor.

The boy beside Sam flung himself down and tried to lap it up. Dinka laughed.

Sam shouted angrily and tried to dodge to one side as the small rebel jabbed him in the ribs with his rifle. The other two village children shrank away. Sam felt them tugging this way and that on the rope, like so many hooked fish. One of them began to sob and then cry, loudly.

'Shut up!' Sam shouted. And deliberately stared Dinka in the eye. He felt strangely disembodied. As if he was a ghost. Or a forest spirit, high up in the branches of a tree, looking down on them all. His hands were still free. It wasn't much, not up against an AK-47. But he had an overpowering urge to seize Dinka by the throat and shake the life out of him.

But even as he went for the boy, something very hard crashed against his head and knocked him sideways. The next thing he knew, he was sprawled full length on the ground. How long did he lie there? Probably only for a few seconds at the most. It felt like an age. His head whirled. His jaw felt loose. There was a loud booming noise from somewhere close. It took him time to realise it was a man's voice, shouting at him to get up. A huge hand gripped him by the arm and swung him to his feet. Captain Simba put his face very close to Sam's.

Sam looked into the man's bloodshot eyes and knew fear. His mouth went dry. His body started to shake. He couldn't stop it. Simba held him by the neck, like a puppy. There was a bubble of saliva at the corner of the man's mouth that bobbled up and down as he spoke. His voice was throaty with menace.

'Show respect, village boy.'

Sam stared at him. Helpless.

'Or else, you dead!'

Sam could smell the man's breath on his face.

Simba glared. 'Dinka here has killed more men than you've got teeth. And you only a boy.'

Then he relaxed his grip. 'What you called?'

Sam told him.

Captain Simba nodded and went on staring at him. 'Well, you're a strong boy, I'll give you that. Might do well.'

He pushed Sam from him. 'But only if you show respect. Otherwise, you just bush meat.' He laughed and the other rebels joined in.

He turned to Dinka and wagged a finger. 'I tell you, Dinka. I don't want this boy killed. Not yet.' Something struck him as funny. He laughed and put an arm around Dinka's shoulders. 'But watch him! Or he'll take your job one of these days. Now, get their feet to the ground. There's a long way to go.'

It was still gloomy in the forest as Sam and the other village children lined up along the narrow game track. It was not long after dawn and the sun was still too low to penetrate the tree tops. The child soldiers ran up and down, pushing the village children into line and cursing at them to hurry up. Sam bent down and picked up the tin of cooking oil. He staggered as he brought it up to chest level. How could he carry something as heavy as this for another whole day? He groaned as the muscles in his arms and shoulders knotted in protest.

He was barefoot, the backs of his heels scraped and raw from yesterday. His new pair of trainers lay close by, half buried in leaf mould. He knew he would never wear them again. At some point, one of the rebels was bound to steal them from him and besides, they'd get in the way when he was marching. There was no point carrying them round his neck. He wondered what the monkeys crashing through the branches overhead would make of them. Perhaps someone would find them. An army patrol might. His father could even be in it. He'd be bound to recognise them and give chase.

The patrol might even now be close behind. Sam savoured the thought.

One of the captured girls was having similar problems. She was trying to get into her old pair of plimsolls. Sam remembered she had been nursing her feet all last night. She managed to pull one halfway on then yelled in pain. She flung the shoe away and threw herself down, weeping bitterly. A small rebel kicked her in the side. The girl did not move. The rebel shouted and yanked at her plaits. Furious, the girl got up and slapped him across the face. The boy's camouflage cap fell off. He looked about seven years old.

For a moment, the sound of the slap hung in the air, before being blown away by a burst of gunfire from Dinka's AK-47. The girl crumpled and fell. The small rebel screamed at her and also fired. Everyone could hear the thump-thump of bullets hitting the ground.

'Untie the bitch!' Dinka shouted. He swung around, pointing his rifle at Sam and then the others. 'You people try anything else and that's what you get. Now, march!'

They stumbled past the girl's body, snatching horrified glances at the corpse. It lay on its side, eyes wide open in surprise. Soon, the ants would find her. And the wasps. Sam didn't want to think about it. He put his head down until all he could see were the legs of the boy in front of him. He kept them there. Making eye contact again with someone like Dinka was a bad idea. He hugged the tin of oil close to his body. It was going to be a long, horrible day. In total silence, they plodded on.

CHAPTER 7

Captain Simba was in a good mood. He slashed at the vegetation on either side of the trail with a stick and had to stop himself whistling or singing snatches of a song. *Only one more night in this spooky forest*, he was thinking. *Maybe this will be the last time I ever come here*. The place gave him the creeps. An entire army could be hiding a couple of metres away and you'd never know it. On either side of the trail, bushes grew head high. It was like walking along an endless green corridor. After a while, you felt you were about to slip off the edge of the world. You had to rub your eyes to keep them properly focused.

Then there were all the strange noises and calls from animals no one ever saw. There was a certain type of monkey that screamed like a woman in pain.

It sent shivers down his back whenever he heard it. Worst of all, he could feel eyes watching him, following his every move. The forest was haunted, of that he was certain. You only had to see how the children's eyes were big with fear and the way they kept looking over their shoulders to know. He licked his lips and tried to be positive. That's what Colonel Dada had told him to be. A leader must be positive at all times. God wanted it that way. So now he concentrated fully on *being positive*.

He'd be home by noon the next day. 'Home' meant hot food and cold beer in the evening with his friends Sekou and Idi. And a soft bed at night. Hot food was something he particularly missed. He refused to allow cooking while out on patrol. Or making a fire for any reason at all. The smell of smoke was unmistakable. An enemy would know exactly what it meant. And where to look.

He'd have to give a full report to Colonel Dada when he got in, but he was used to that. And to dealing with the man's sudden rages, of course. Of the five other adult soldier 'Unit Commanders', he could handle Dada better than anyone. And, after all, he was bringing in twelve more healthy children to do God's work.

No. Not twelve, he corrected himself. *Only eleven,*

now. An owl gave a shrill cry and flew out of a bush in front of him. Horrified, Captain Simba stopped and stared after it. Any owl seen in daytime meant bad luck. This one had flown from left to right across his path. He couldn't remember just how dangerous that might be. For sure, though, it was an ill omen. He'd tell Colonel Dada about it and ask for his special protection. The Colonel's spirit was strong. Stronger than anything Captain Simba might meet in the forest.

He resumed marching and thought about the girl lying dead back there. What a pity. She had hit one of his children hard across the face and Dinka had shot her. Well, what did she expect? These village youngsters were so ignorant and badly behaved. No! The tragedy was that she would have made someone a good wife.

He shook his head. Silly girl! It was such a stupid thing to do. Still, some good might come of it. It would certainly warn the others not to fool around. That big boy. What was his name? Sam! Yes, him. The one with much too much spirit. He could do with learning a really big lesson. And soon!

Captain Simba walked on at a steady pace. Not so fast as to exhaust the smaller village children but quickly enough to make sure they would all sleep soundly when night came. He would give them food and water tonight. Nothing much. Some slices of cold, boiled cassava and a handful of ground nuts. Just enough to keep them going and give them a bit of encouragement.

Later, Captain Simba thought about Sam a little more. He had mixed feelings about him. Sam was the type of boy who could go either way. Dinka had been the same. This Sam might make a very good rebel. But then he might not. So perhaps the shooting was a good thing after all. Teach him a lesson. Anyway, he'd give the boy time and a proper chance to show what he was made of. If he was still unsure of him then, he could always ask the Colonel for advice. If anyone knew about boys, it was Colonel Dada. And grown men too. *Look how he picked me*, he thought. And smiled, proudly.

Before the rebels had come to his little town, he had been the boatman there. Every day, he'd rowed people back and forth across the river and kept a keen eye out for crocodiles. There had been one as long as his boat. No one in the town had known him as 'Simba' then, and he hadn't been any sort of captain either. Everyone had called him Eugene. He didn't seem to have a surname.

The day the rebels came, he remembered rowing to

the far bank to keep out of harm's way. He had never heard heavy automatic gunfire before. As the battle raged for control of the rubbish-choked streets, he had stayed in his boat, thrilled by the sound of fighting. He had never heard anything so exciting in all his life.

The government-backed forces were outnumbered. There were only twenty of them in the town to begin with. As the sound of firing came steadily closer, he had stood up in the boat, shouting and whooping encouragement. He joined in the fighting with an imaginary gun and ducked and dodged hostile fire. The boat rocked under him and little wavelets splashed up along the bank.

In the mid afternoon, three soldiers and a sergeant rushed on to the jetty on the opposite bank, frantically shouting at him to come and get them. He remembered admiring the three white stripes on the sergeant's arm. He was just about to start rowing when a line of children appeared, firing from the hip. Some were in green combat uniforms. Most of them wore ordinary, coloured T-shirts. Their demented screaming was like a thousand parrots fighting.

The last remaining soldier knelt and fired at them. Then he jumped into the river and struck out across the chocolate-coloured water. From the corner of his eye, Eugene had caught movement further down the river and then watched an ominous V-shaped ripple, moving steadily out towards midstream.

Later, the rebels had called him over and their leader, Colonel Dada, congratulated him on his presence of mind in staying put. Eugene did not know what 'presence of mind' was. But he had smiled happily. Colonel Dada also told him that the children were doing God's work and that he too could be saved. When they had suggested he join them, he had nodded enthusiastically.

It was a happy outcome for them all. The boatman soon discovered he was a natural soldier. He had an instinctive grasp of tactics. He could also take a jammed machine gun to pieces, clear the blockage and reassemble the weapon in less than ninety seconds. He was not only physically strong but fiercely ambitious as well. In short, as Colonel Dada quickly realised, he was a natural to play the part of 'Captain Simba'.

Now, Captain Simba smiled up at the green canopy above his head. He was doing God's work and it felt good. Really good. Then, his smile faded. He'd better check to see what Dinka and the rest of the child soldiers were up to. He did not want any more village children killed or hurt before he paraded them in front of the Colonel. Dinka could be a nasty bit of work if you didn't keep him under firm control.

With a sigh, Captain Simba stood to one side and watched the unhappy procession stumble past. None of them looked grateful. But then, they never did.

CHAPTER 8

Sam sat up cautiously and looked around. No one else seemed to be awake. Overhead, the forest was alive with bird song. Some unknown animals were calling to one another and he wondered what they were. The village children were huddled tightly together. They had gone to sleep with the big ones in the middle. During the night, though, some of the others had managed to wiggle their way in between. They now lay packed together like so many fish.

There was a reason for this. Fear! They were all frightened of the forest. Even in daytime, it was gloomy and sinister. A child could get lost here very quickly and never be seen again. It was an alien place, far removed from the sunshine and space they were used to. But there was one particular horror that stalked their imaginations. Snakes.

They had all heard stories of the snakes which lived on the forest floor. Unseen and unmoving, until your foot went too close. But even more terrible was what happened during the night when these snakes came gliding out of their hiding places to find you and lie beside you, to share your warmth.

There was one snake in particular they dreaded. They were too frightened to even whisper its name among themselves, in case the evil forest spirits heard. But everyone knew it to be 'Nene Nyoka' – the thick snake. It had a heavy, wedge-shaped body and was covered in pink, brown and black blotches for camouflage. In the dappled light of the forest floor it was impossible to see. Its fangs grew to over three centimetres in length. They were long and curved and if they bit you, they would not let go until you were dead.* And that was why Sam sat perfectly still until he was satisfied there was nothing close by.

He heard shouting and recognised Dinka's voice. Anger surged up inside him. The sound of the boy's voice drove everything else from his mind. One day, he would kill Dinka. One day, he would avenge what these people had done to his mother and his sisters. To

---

* Probably a gaboon viper.

himself and his family. He banged his fists on the ground and fought to keep his feelings under control. He must stop making an enemy of Dinka. The boy had the power of life and death over him. Simba had made that very clear. Sam remembered the girl with the shoe and what had happened to her. From now on, he must be cunning and wait for the right time to escape. First though, he had to hide his feelings. If he didn't, he wouldn't survive long.

'Box clever, Sam, his father used to tell him. 'Never show how you really feel. Then you got surprise on your side!'

A group of child soldiers appeared. As Sam got to his feet, they began kicking the village children awake. Sam's mouth formed a grin. A moment later, he turned away and busied himself with the tin of cooking oil. They stood in the rain as the rebels gave them a handful of peanuts each and allowed them one swig of water. Then it was time to march.

The first hundred metres were the worst. Sam groaned out loud as he hobbled forward on bruised feet. After that, as long as he kept his brain occupied, it wasn't too bad. There were ways of forgetting the pain. Yesterday, he had played complicated football matches in his mind, using the different coloured beetles he saw to represent goals scored. He had gone all the way to a cup final before getting bored.

Today, he thought, would be easier. He had overheard two of the rebels saying it was only going to be a five-hour march. So, slowly, like an old caterpillar, the column wound its way towards the rebel's main camp.

Sometime later they came to a sudden halt. Taken by surprise, the village children bumped into each other and, for the first time in days, they laughed. Furious, the child soldiers pointed their guns at them. They put their fingers to their lips and made angry shushing motions.

'What's happening, Mr Dinka, sir?' Sam asked very respectfully.

Dinka ignored him and walked to the back of the column. But when they started marching again, he returned and paused beside Sam. 'Checking it's clear,' he grunted and strode on. A smile spread across Sam's face. He wasn't entirely clear what he had achieved but he had done something. Of that he was certain.

They came out of the forest unexpectedly. From darkness to blinding light in only twenty paces. They came to a ragged halt and everyone stood there, blinking in the sunshine. Someone even raised a feeble cheer. It felt wonderful. Like a cleansing bath. Sam turned and grinned at the boy behind. The rebels were also pleased. They chattered amongst themselves until Captain Simba told them to march on.

The ground in front of them descended in a series of ridges that spread away to the horizon. Everywhere Sam looked, he could see clumps of flat-topped fever trees, yellow elephant grass and anthills. A range of low hills cut across the middle of the scene and Sam guessed there was a river running there. Feeling almost happy, he started to hum. An hour or so later, they came to a dirt road. The rebels looked much more relaxed. Most of them now carried their rifles casually across the back of their shoulders. Sam guessed they were getting close.

Without hesitation, they crossed the road. Sam thought he saw a set of recent tyre marks but couldn't be sure. Soon they came to a well worn track. Puffs of dust rose under their feet and settled on the grass on either side. The track began to lead uphill. Sam put his head down and concentrated on this final effort. As they reached the top of the hill, he saw buildings ahead – low buildings, half hidden in the trees.

They looked like old government school buildings or even mission stations. Not unlike the hospital his mother had once walked him to, ten kilometres from his village. Originally, they had been painted white. Now, splashes of mud from many rainy seasons had stained them a faded red. It had to be the rebel's camp.

There was a sand-bagged watchtower at the entrance, manned by two adult rebel soldiers. They shouted something to Captain Simba and all three of them started to laugh. Sam could see their grins fifty metres away. Dinka fired into the air and gave a loud whoop. The next moment, a swarm of child soldiers came running towards them. They all had an AK-47 slung over their shoulders. Most of them were dressed in new-looking combat kit. Uniforms that were far too big for them. The smaller ones had rolled up their trousers while their jackets hung down around their knees.

Captain Simba gave a bellow of pleasure, stooped and swept up two of the children. The others crowded around him, dancing with excitement. Sam stared at them in contempt. He had never seen such a ragbag collection of individuals in his life before. His father would have a fit if he saw this lot, he thought, remembering the care he took with his uniform. But as he reached the watchtower, a shiver ran down his back. Around the camp boundary there were human skulls impaled on wooden stakes as far as he could see.

They went past the watchtower and the end of the nearest building, then into an open compound beyond. It was the size of a football pitch and reminded Sam of a parade ground. There were similar buildings evenly spaced around its perimeter and clumps of feathery palm trees in between. There were groups of child soldiers squatting in the dust and, at the far end, others were kicking a football around.

Captain Simba shouted an order and they all wheeled around and followed him towards a raised platform where there was a solitary chair. Sam craned his neck to see. His first thought was that it was more like a throne than a chair. Someone was sitting there, surrounded by large, brightly-coloured cushions.

Captain Simba ordered them to line up in front of the dais, then he turned and saluted smartly. The figure stood up. Sam's eyes widened in amazement. The most extraordinary person he had ever seen took a step forward and looked down at him!

CHAPTER 9

The man was very tall. He was dressed like a priest in a long white soutane* that reached down almost to his ankles. On his head he wore a bishop's purple skull cap. Across his chest, a row of medals flashed whenever they caught the sun. In his right hand, he held a large wooden crucifix. Sam stared in horror at the dead bat with outstretched wings that had been nailed there. He also carried an AK-47 over his shoulder with its muzzle pointing downwards.

His eyes were bright and restless. They flicked back and forth over the village children, fixing on an individual for a moment then moving on to the next. His face was long and pinched. *Like a burnt cashew*

* Soutane: A cassock, or long coat often worn by Roman Catholic priests overseas.

nut, Sam thought. The man's gaze settled on him and Sam bowed his head to avoid it.

The man held the cross high in front of him and blessed them in a language Sam had never heard before.

'Alleluja!' cried Captain Simba. He nodded his head vigorously and looked encouragingly at the children nearest to him. Someone mumbled a reply. The tall man, meanwhile, laid the crucifix on the throne, unslung his rifle and fired a short burst into the air. A pair of crows flapped away.

'Alleluja!' the tall man shouted. He had a very deep voice. 'Welcome all of you. Welcome!' He rested the butt of his rifle on his hip and smiled down at them. 'Praise God who has brought you here to do His work.'

'Alleluja!' Captain Simba encouraged.

'With God and our guns we will scatter His enemies for ever,' the man went on. He bent down and peered at the children. 'Do you know who I am?' he asked.

The children shuffled their feet and wondered if this was some sort of a trap. Sam stared hard at the ground. No one made a sound.

Above them the man shouted, 'I am Colonel Dada the Merciful. God's chosen instrument. I am your friend and protector. Look at me!'

Captain Simba hurried along the line of children,

tapping them under the chin until they were all staring up at Colonel Dada. Sam sneaked a quick look behind him. Dinka was lounging there, picking his teeth with a fingernail. He did not seem over-impressed by what was happening.

Colonel Dada spread his hands over the children. 'You are now part of my family. I am your father and your mother. God has chosen you to be with me. You are very fortunate. Do what you are told and you will be well looked after.'

He slung the rifle back over his shoulder and looked at Captain Simba. 'Their new life starts today. Take them to their quarters. And see they eat and drink.'

He leaped lightly down from the platform. In the awed silence that followed, Sam heard his medals clinking as he walked towards a waiting crowd of child soldiers. They parted respectfully to let him through. Colonel Dada rubbed some of their heads as he strode past. Nearby, two dogs started to snarl at each other and the child soldiers whooped and ran to form a circle around them.

'You all come with me,' Captain Simba ordered. 'I'll show you your hut and your bed roll. You'll be sharing the room with the rest of my children. Now all Captain Simba's boys are together. They are senior soldiers to you. So show respect! Your training starts tomorrow. Very early. Get some food and a lot of sleep. And remember, you now belong to Colonel Dada!'

CHAPTER 10

Sam's father – 'Tembo', as he was affectionately known – was worried. The Sergeant Major had sent for him twenty minutes ago. Now, he stood outside his commanding officer's door waiting to be marched in.

'The Captain wants to see you, Corporal Mbali,' the Sergeant had told him quietly. 'He'll tell you what it's about.' And he'd refused to meet Tembo's eye.

Tembo racked his brains. Why would the officer want to talk to him? He had done nothing wrong that he could think of. Nothing at all. And nor had any of the eight soldiers in his section. Life had been very quiet since he had returned from home leave, a week ago. So whatever this was about, it must have happened whilst he was away. Having reached this conclusion, he relaxed a little.

A platoon of new recruits was being drilled on the main square in front of him. A smartly turned out drill sergeant was teaching them how to salute. 'Longest way up . . . shortest way down,' he was shouting.

Tembo watched their efforts and smiled. He remembered doing exactly the same thing when he had been a rookie, ten years ago. On this same parade ground. The British had built the camp many years ago. They had called it Templar Barracks. Nothing much had changed in the intervening years except the name. It was now called Freedom Barracks but the long wooden buildings with their neatly cut patches of grass and the white painted stones alongside the square were unchanged. Tembo liked things to stay the same. It gave life a sense of continuity.

The door beside him opened and Captain Mbote himself called him in. Tembo frowned. This was most unusual. It was the Sergeant Major's job to march everyone in and out. What on earth had happened? And then, when the officer told him to sit down in the one armchair, his hands began to shake.

The Captain looked at him for a moment. Then, choosing his words carefully, he said, 'I'm afraid I've got some very bad news for you, Corporal Mbali.'

Tembo swallowed. He noticed that the Sergeant Major had also come in and was standing close beside him. He sat very still and concentrated on what the Captain was saying.

'We've had reports earlier this morning that the God's Freedom Army has been attacking villages in the east of the country.'

Tembo looked at him in horror.

'I'm afraid to say that your village, Tshombe, was one of them.'

'No!' Tembo cried out. He stared wild-eyed at the Captain. 'But my wife . . . my kids! That's where they are! No!'

The Captain's voice deepened. 'A police patrol has found the bodies of many adults, both men and women. But some of the children are missing. I think we all know what that means.'

He sat back unhappily and watched Tembo put his face in his hands. The Sergeant Major put his hand on Tembo's shoulder and gripped it tight.

Captain Mbote came from behind his desk and helped Tembo get to his feet. 'We'll catch the devils!' he told him, angrily. 'We'll get them. And when we do, we'll hang them from the tallest tree we can find!'

CHAPTER 11

Sam squatted on his haunches and hung his head. He was alone. His eyes closed and his chest rose and fell as he battled to stop himself crying out loud. Outside the Simba Boys' hut, a football match was being played. Judging by the noise, it was an important game. Sam heard the catcalls and the shouts as if in a dream. He had no idea who was involved and cared even less. His own demons and homesickness were engulfing him.

He was reliving the last time he had seen his mother's face as they marched him away. He remembered, too, the lazy brown smoke curling up into the sky and the shootings. He knew what they meant. She was dead. He was sure of it. Shot down like a dog in her own village. With a groan he clutched at his head and started to rock backwards and forwards.

Captain Simba and Dinka had brought them here to their hut earlier in the day. Dinka had tossed them all a blanket from a pile just inside the door.

'This is your place,' Captain Simba had told them. 'All my boys live and sleep here. Together.' Near the door, there were a number of camp beds laid out in neat rows. He pointed to them. 'Those beds belong to the senior children. Maybe you'll all have one someday. Maybe not.'

Silently, Sam had spread his blanket on the floor and looked around. The room was a long one with a low ceiling. Sunlight poured in through the holes in the corrugated iron roof. The floor was concrete and worn. The windows had all been nailed over with pieces of wood. There was no furniture of any kind in there.

'You want food?' Dinka called. 'Any of you hungry? Come with me!'

Sam had joined the rush. The ache in his stomach was suddenly the only thing that mattered. Dinka walked fifty metres beyond the hut with them, pointed out the cookhouse beside a clump of trees, and turned away. Sam ran with his elbows held wide and pushed his way to the front.

Two women were standing behind a row of cooking pots, talking animatedly. They had looked around and frowned at Sam as he skidded to a halt. As the other village children arrived, they began shouting and waving them away. By now, Sam's mouth was watering uncontrollably.

'You too late!' one woman called.

'And where your bowls?' the other demanded. 'No bowls, no food.'

Bowls? Sam blinked. He had taken a step forward. 'Please Ma'am,'* he'd said as politely as he could. 'We'd just got here. We've got nothing. We've not had food for days.'

The women looked cross. 'Who's your boss?' the older one demanded.

'Captain Simba,' he had told her. 'And Dinka told us to come here. Sorry,' he'd added, doing his best to smile.

Reluctantly, the younger woman had found and handed out some old aluminium plates. When they ran out, they both rummaged around and produced some empty tin cans.

'You lucky,' she told Sam.

'You wait till I see your boss,' the other grumbled. She began ladling stew and mealies from a cooking pot on to their plates.

* Ma'am: In East Africa, this is a polite greeting given to older women by younger men and boys.

'Don't eat too quick, none of you,' the younger one warned. 'Your bellies ain't like they was. They much smaller now.'

'If you eat too quick, it'll all come up,' agreed the other.

Sam had been too hungry to listen. The food was delicious. As good as anything . . . as anything . . . his mother had made. The thought had made him pause guiltily, then he was sucking at his fingers and going back for more.

'You not listen to a word I say,' the younger woman chided. She put a heavy iron lid back on the pot. 'No more till tonight. Get some more then.'

'Thank you, Ma'am,' Sam said.

The woman frowned for a moment then smiled at him. Sam had felt his eyes fill with tears. He looked away quickly and swallowed the sensation deep inside him.

She watched him. 'You get some sleep now. You look very tired.'

He had mumbled his thanks.

'You bring your bowl next time,' the older one had called after him.

Later, as the noise of the football match surged in and out of the hut, Sam gave himself up to misery. His body ached. His feet were bruised and raw in patches. He was exhausted. He lay down on his blanket but his brain refused to let him sleep. He found himself thinking about Captain Simba. What was it he had said?

'*You belong to Colonel Dada now.*'

Sam thought about this with growing anger. Did Simba mean 'belong' in the same way a person is a prisoner in jail? Or in the way a goat or a cow 'belong' to a human being? Or even as a slave belongs to his master!

The full realisation had Sam sitting bolt upright. 'No!' he shouted in rage. 'Never! I'm *not* Dada's slave!'

Someone was standing in the doorway, watching him. He must have heard everything Sam had said.

CHAPTER 12

The boy in the doorway came slowly into the room. He was small, thin, impish-looking and wore a bright green T-shirt. Sam's words seemed to hang in the air between them. Would the boy tell Colonel Dada what he'd just said? Would they shoot him straight away or lock him up and kill him later? Sweat gathered on Sam's face.

The boy said nothing, but his eyes never left Sam. He unslung the AK-47 from his shoulder and laid it on the floor. Then he walked into the middle of the room and did two perfect handstands in quick succession. Next, he retrieved his gun, went over to a nearby camp bed, and sat down on it.

Sam's mouth dropped open. He watched the boy in silence. He appeared quite unconcerned. As Sam stared, the boy pulled a rag from his back pocket and began to clean his rifle.

Then he looked up and met Sam's gaze. 'Ever had one of these before?'

Sam gulped and shook his head. For once, lost for words.

'But you know what it is?'

'It's an AK-47,' Sam told him, 'I think.'

The boy nodded. 'Best gun in the world. You can drop it in a river, get it covered with mud or sand, and it still fires.'

'My dad's in the Army. He's a corporal. He's got a machine gun.'

The boy shrugged. 'Lucky him! Well, let me tell you something. He's not had as much action as we have.' And he patted the gun almost affectionately.

Sam thought about this. 'You been fighting?'

'Sure thing. We had to get out in a hurry, mind. The other lot were too strong for us. Dada ran around like a headless chicken.' He broke off and chuckled.

'What other lot?' Sam asked.

'General Ublique and his boys, of course. There are two times more of them than us.'

'General Ublique? Who's he?'

'Some other crazy! He and Dada hate each other.

He's sworn to crucify Dada if he ever catches him.' He looked at Sam. 'You're really new here. Did Simba bring you in?'

Sam nodded. 'This morning.'

The boy laughed. 'Poor old Simba! He wants to be a proper soldier – only somehow he's ended up here with us. Anyway, welcome! You're one of Simba's boys now. In his own little army. God help us.'

A silence fell between them which Sam was suddenly keen to fill.

'Where were you fighting?'

'Up in Rwanda. We had a nice little gold-digging thing going. Then General Ubique heard about it and decided he wanted it.' He went to the door, lifted the AK-47 and squinted up the barrel. 'That's better,' he said. He put the gun back on his bed and came across to Sam and squatted down opposite.

'A lot of our children got killed up there,' he said.

'Children—?' Sam began to ask.

The boy interrupted. 'You, me and all those poor little people you hear outside. We're all Dada's children. Alleluja! Unless we go join General Ubique instead.' He suddenly looked Sam in the eye. 'You ain't a spy, are you?'

Sam gasped. 'A spy? Who for?'

The boy shook his head. 'Who knows? Dada . . .

Simba . . . They all think I'm a bit strange. I don't fit in here.'

'Who'd want to?' said Sam hotly. 'I can't wait to get out.'

The boy laughed and stuck out a hand. 'I'm Kito. I been here too long. Now, I got to go and do something you can't help me with.'

He stood beside Sam. 'Where the others you came with?'

'Outside. Watching the football.'

'Hoping to make nice, new friends.' Kito shook his head. 'They won't. You can't make friends with scorpions.'

He bent towards Sam and lowered his voice. 'Take your time,' he warned. 'This place is like nothing you've seen before. Keep your mouth tight shut. Remember, we're all killers in here.' Then he grinned and slapped Sam on the shoulder. 'I'll keep an eye on you if you like.'

He pulled out a crumpled pack of cigarettes and offered one. Sam hesitated then shook his head.

'See you around,' Kito said casually. He winked at Sam and left.

CHAPTER 13

'Forty-eight . . . forty-nine . . . Come on, young Sam! Go for it!' Captain Simba shouted. 'One more and then you can stop!'

Sam closed his eyes and forced himself to do the final press-up. He could feel the sweat running across his naked chest and down under his ribs. He gave a loud groan as his shaking arms collapsed and he fell on to the uncaring ground. The blood was roaring inside his head. His lungs were bursting and he no longer cared about anything. They could kill him if they liked. He was going to stay here for ever and let the dust he was lying in turn to mud.

By Sam's reckoning, he had been here for five days. Days of non-stop physical activity. Three times a day there were runs through the surrounding bush. Then there was the assault course, where they climbed over rocks and squeezed through half-buried oil drums. This was followed by army-style drill. Sam knew that he was stronger and fitter than he had ever been. And much more mentally alert. He ate well and was getting used to sleeping on the concrete floor. If he hadn't been a prisoner, he might have even started to enjoy it. But for him, it was only a means to an end. For a start, he was determined to be stronger and tougher than Dinka.

A sharp prod from Captain Simba's boot brought him back to the present, in a rush.

'On your feet!'

Sam did as he was told and joined the others waiting nearby. Captain Simba stood in front of them, legs apart. He was dressed in a pair of sand-coloured combat trousers and a white singlet. He was very muscular.

'We'll do a kilometre run then you can fall out and go back to your hut.'

Later, after supper, Kito nodded to him and jerked a thumb at the door.

'Feel like a walk?'

They went outside and made their way slowly around the compound. There were the usual groups of

79

child soldiers playing cards or dice and arguing loudly. The adult soldiers who manned the outside watchtower smoked and listened to some far away pop station. The reception came and went in waves but they seemed happy enough.

'Simba was really bad today,' said Sam. 'He thinks he's Superman.'

Kito gave a little grin. 'That's why he leaves us senior children alone most of the time. Too busy making you new boys into soldiers. Thank you, kind sir!' and he bowed from the waist in mock gratitude.

Sam scratched his head. Kito had a different sense of humour from anyone he had ever known. Sometimes he didn't quite know how to take it.

'Still,' Kito went on, 'there are worse men than Simba in this place.'

Sam looked at him with interest.

Kito stopped and brought out a small tin. 'Chewing tobacco,' he explained. 'Want some?' He popped a piece into his mouth and held out the tin.

Sam peered at it suspiciously. 'You like this better than cigarettes?'

Kito made a face. 'It's different.'

They walked out into the bush. In front of them, lizards scuttled away and hid under the thorn bushes.

'Simba's a crazy man,' Kito continued. 'He's crazy

80

to be a proper soldier. Others here are crazy for drugs. Some just like the killing. Can't think why none of the children ain't shot them yet.'

'Maybe they're all afraid of their bosses.'

Kito considered this. 'Maybe. Or maybe they're just too stupid to know what's good for them.'

Sam looked sideways at Kito. For a moment he hesitated, then, taking a deep breath, he said, 'Who's Colonel Dada?'

Instinctively, Kito looked over his shoulder. 'Dada the Merciful is the big boss,' he said quietly. 'And the biggest crazy. He's the lifelong president of the Dead Boys' Club. He's like God to everyone else.'

'But not you and me,' Sam told him.

Kito grabbed at Sam's arm. 'You don't say that out loud. Ever. You hear me, Sam!' he scolded. 'You want to stay alive?'

Sam bowed his head and they walked on towards a line of fever trees.

Kito licked his lips. 'People say Dada was a priest in Uganda. Then he went wrong. Became mad. Thought he was God's right hand man here on earth. He saw visions. They told him what to do and where to go. He still does. Then he gathers all the children together and tells them that it's the will of Heaven. Or some such. And we all obey.'

Sam nodded slowly. 'But all these children. And men like Simba. Why do they follow him? What are they doing here?'

Kito waved away a wasp. 'They're Dada's loyal followers,' he said bitterly. 'They do what he says without question. And he pays them with drugs and guns and wives. Depends what they want. They rob and steal for him. It's easier than being a farmer. God's Freedom Army.' He laughed, bitterly.

They continued on in silence for a while.

'When the men get short of children,' Kito said quietly, 'they go and steal some more. New children, like me and you. Happens all the time. Especially when they're busy.'

'Busy?' Sam asked.

Kito nodded. 'Busy stealing money, ambushing other children, running gold diggings. Whatever Dada wants.'

Sam listened in gloomy silence. Finally, he shook his head. 'I can't stay here,' he told Kito. 'I got to get out.'

Kito slapped him hard across the back. 'You crazy!' he shouted.

Sam gave a yell and spun round to face him. 'That hurt!' he snapped. 'What you do that for? Don't *you* want to go home?'

Kito spat out a stream of tobacco juice. 'Of course I want to go home! But where do I go? My village is all burned down. No person lives there any more.'

He put a hand over his eyes and said nothing for a moment. Then he shook his head. 'Some of the new children try to run home. They always get caught. You want to know what happens when they catch you? You'll see soon enough.'

By now, the sun was dipping down towards the horizon. 'Better get back,' Kito warned. 'They also think you a runaway if you get into camp after dark.'

Back inside the compound, they separated. Slowly, Sam headed for his hut. Kito was totally different from everyone else there. He was not that much older than Sam but so much more savvy about life. But could he trust him? He hoped so. Perhaps between the two of them, they could find a way out of here, after all.

As Sam lay down on his blanket, Captain Simba came into the room. He made his usual quick head count and left with a cheery wave.

'See you in the morning, Simba Boys!' he called, grinning.

CHAPTER 14

'OK, Simba Boys! Come to me . . . NOW!' Captain Simba shouted. He turned to face the runners, flinging out his arms in a gesture for them to gather round. Gratefully, they staggered towards him. Some of them collapsed and lay panting in the dust.

'Don't you dare lie down!' Captain Simba roared. 'Get up!' He kicked their feet. 'You got thirty seconds to get your breath back.' He held up an arm and stared pointedly at his watches.

Sam took a deep breath and held it for as long as he could. He did this several times until his heartbeat became almost normal again. Then he looked at Simba and wondered what was coming next. He could see that the man was very pleased about something.

Captain Simba put his hands on his hips and smiled

around at them. 'Now, I'm happy to tell you,' he began, 'that because you been good students and have worked hard, Colonel Dada and me got a big surprise for you.'

Sam looked at the faces of the other children. They were all fixed intently on Captain Simba. He had never come across the expression 'father figure' before but, despite this, he was aware of a change in their attitude towards the man. They were beginning to crave his approval. There was even a growing sense of anticipation about what would happen next.

'Tomorrow,' Captain Simba told them, 'you getting your own gun! An AK-47 for every one of you. And then we'll show you how to use it!'

There was a buzz of excitement amongst the village children. They began chattering and nodding. Then someone cheered! Captain Simba beamed and slapped a hand against his thigh in delight. 'Dinka will come round after supper and give out the ammunition. He'll show you how to load the bullets.'

The boy beside Sam let out a whoop and gave him a friendly punch on the arm. Sam lifted his fist and scowled. He was shocked by their enthusiasm. He forced himself to put on his usual smile but it took an effort. He looked at them in disbelief. They'd all seen what bullets and a gun could do. He wanted to shout

out and remind them of the girl they had left behind in the forest. The girl Dinka had shot. They'd all been there for that, hadn't they? And walked past her body. Yet here they were, cheering like a bunch of silly kids. It didn't make any sense.

'So everyone stay in the hut when supper ends,' Captain Simba was telling them. 'Meantime, anyone who wants to take a bath can come with me! I'll be lookout!' He held up his rifle and pretended to fire it.

They cheered again and ran after him along the track that led to the river. Sam let himself be carried along. He was aware of Dinka running beside him but didn't say anything. He was too stunned.

The river was shallow and full of rocks and clumps of reed. Perfect cover for the crocodiles who watched and waited there. No one was allowed by the river unless someone with a rifle went with them. Twice a day, the women gathered and went there, carrying tall water pots on their heads. The different huts took it in turns to protect them. The same happened when there was laundry to do.

Sam hung back as they reached the riverbank. He was terrified of crocodiles. They attacked ferociously and without warning. He had once seen a dog taken by one. He'd been standing near a water hole not far from his village, when a dog trotted up to drink. A crocodile had reared up out of the placid water and seized the dog by its nose. It led the dog almost gently out into the middle of the water, then flung it over its back and rolled on top of it, crushing the air from the dog's lungs.

Sam had run from the water hole as if all the devils in Africa were after him and he had never told his parents what had happened. He remembered it now and shivered. Beside him, the other children laughed and sat in their underpants, happily splashing water over each other.

'Not going in, young Sam?' Captain Simba asked. His dark glasses caught the sun and Sam had a momentary glimpse of himself, sitting on a rock looking very solemn.

'No, Boss!' he replied, feeling confused. He didn't want to talk to this man and he didn't want him to know about his fear of the river. So he lied instead. 'Just thinking about firing my rifle tomorrow, Boss.'

Captain Simba grinned down at him. 'Good boy, Sam! You'll go far. You hear me?'

And Sam, survivor that he was, smiled back and said, 'Thank you, sir!'

* * *

'What's wrong?' Kito asked later that evening. He squatted down beside Sam and put an arm briefly around the boy's shoulders. Sam was shaking.

'You got a fever?' Kito wanted to know and pulled Sam to his feet. 'Better come with me. I can get you some medicine,' he said for the benefit of a couple of other boys in the hut.

Outside, he said urgently, 'Sam, what is it?'

After a while Sam told him. 'I got two loaded magazines in there. On my blanket. Tomorrow I use them. Tomorrow they give me my own gun.' He shook his head. 'I am a fool,' he said. 'I never thought I'd be doing it. Shooting, I mean.'

Kito looked at him in disbelief.

'But Sam, that's why you're here. What other reason is there? That's what Simba's been training you up for.' He rumpled Sam's hair. 'Man! You must know that.'

Sam nodded reluctantly and wiped his nose on his hand. 'I suppose. But I don't want to. I'm going to run away. Tonight.'

Kito seized him by the elbows and shook him. 'Sam. Listen! You got to do it. It's camouflage. *Your* camouflage. If you want to survive this place, you do what they want. That's what your father would say. Right?'

'Maybe.'

They saw a cockroach emerge from the bottom of a wall and run across the ground in front of them. It stopped suddenly, its antennae twitching. 'It's looking at us,' Kito said. He raised a hand and the insect shot back into another crack.

'Now there's a *real* survivor for you,' he told Sam. 'Be more like him.'

CHAPTER 15

'Here you are, Sam! Meet your new best friend!'
Captain Simba grinned and thrust the AK-47 at the
boy. Sam took it with both hands and was surprised
how heavy it was.* For a moment, he felt dazed. He
had never touched a gun like this before. And this gun,
he knew, had already killed many times. Perhaps even
people in his own village. His hands shook a little and
he took a deep breath to steady himself. Captain Simba
was further down the line handing each of them a
weapon. Dinka walked behind, carrying several more
over his shoulder.

There was a sheen of oil over the metal parts and
the barrel felt icy cold. The wooden stock was scarred

* An AK-47 weighs approximately 4.30 kilograms – unloaded.

and chipped and someone had carved their initials on it. Where was that person now? Sam had a sudden memory of the teacher's desk in his village school. That had initials on it as well. The desk was the only piece of furniture in the room. He wondered if Sister Angelica, the teacher from the mission, had managed to escape.

Captain Simba was shouting again. 'Watch me! This is how you load the weapon!'

He held the curved magazine in his left hand and snapped it into place on the underside of the rifle. 'See! Watch! I do it again. Right! All of you . . . Take out an empty magazine . . . Empty . . . Now you do it!'

They practised loading and unloading for the next ten minutes. When Simba was satisfied, he motioned them to spread out. 'Keep at least three metres apart! Dinka! Sort them out!

'Now, take out a loaded magazine this time,' Captain Simba was calling. 'Hold it in your left hand. When I say "Load" you do the same – and . . . LOAD!'

Sam did so. And gasped out loud, as the implication of what he had done came home to him. Here he was, Sam Mbali, holding a loaded rifle in his hands, while the murderers of his family and friends stood less than ten metres away. He could kill them. Just like that. It would be so easy.

'Don't touch the trigger!' Captain Simba roared. 'Not until I tell you to. Dinka! The one at the end there! See what he's doing!'

Sam looked at the others on either side of him. Were they thinking the same thing? The boy on his right grinned at him. His eyes were shining. The one on the other side was wearing a frown of concentration. Sam counted. Nine boys. None of the girls. They must all be in the woman's hut. He remembered Kito telling him, 'They only give the really evil girls a gun. The ones who'd put a bee in your ear, if Colonel Dada told them to.'

Captain Simba was standing off to one side now. Sam gulped and gripped his gun fiercely. He wanted to jump out in front and . . .

'Right! Look at me!' Simba yelled. 'Your weapon will not fire until you slip the safety catch off. See here!'

The safety catch! Sam had forgotten the safety catch! He felt himself go weak at the knees and almost drop the gun. He started coughing to cover his panic. If he had leaped out and confronted Dinka or Simba, and raised his gun to shoot them, he would be dead by now. Lying right here, his life-blood draining away.

Quite unaware of all this, Captain Simba pointed at a line of mango trees twenty metres in front of them. 'I want you to hit those trees for me. Ready? Safety catches. OFF. And . . . FIRE!'

The command was drowned by the volley of gunfire. In a trance, Sam pushed the safety catch to 'off' and pulled the trigger. The rifle juddered in his hands. The muzzle drooped and he saw the ground in front of him kick up in little sprays of earth.

Then Captain Simba was standing beside him, shouting in his ear.

'Hold the gun like I showed you, stupid!'

Sam remembered. He held the gun at waist height and jammed the wooden stock between the side of his stomach and the inside of his elbow. He saw Simba nod his head up and down vigorously and then point forward at the trees. Sam braced himself, squeezed the trigger again, and saw pieces of bark and white scraps of wood explode in all directions. The tree shivered and seemed to slip to one side. He heard someone laughing with excitement and realised it was him.

His nostrils were full of the stink of cordite fumes. Fantastic vibrations were pounding up and down his spine. He was shouting at the top of his voice. Here was power. Real strength. He felt invincible. He wanted more! And then there was only the dull click of an empty magazine. A wave of disgust flooded over him.

He saw Captain Simba clap his hands together and

do a little jig of pleasure. 'Never fails!' Simba was shouting. 'Better than a spliff, eh, Dinka?'

Sam watched Dinka walk behind the line of gunners towards him. He was chewing on a matchstick. He raised a lazy hand in Captain Simba's direction but said nothing. His face was expressionless.

Now Captain Simba was shouting more orders. In a daze, Sam struggled to obey.

'Put your weapons on the ground and stand back from them!' Captain Simba boomed. 'And gather around me!'

They ran towards him, jostling each other to be the nearest.

'Everyone enjoy that?' Simba demanded, looking down at their nodding heads. 'Now let me tell you something. I'm going to make proper soldiers of you. *Real* soldiers. Good enough to join the rest of my boys. But, to be good enough, you got to practise. And we're going to start doing that . . . tomorrow!'

The children cheered. Dinka cleared his throat and spat. Sam slipped away behind a bush and was sick.

That night, lying on his blanket in the dark, Sam relived the day. The episode with the safety catch had almost been a disaster. He was lucky to still be alive. In future he was going to 'box clever'. His father's face swam into his memory. It was an omen, and the thought cheered him.

From now on, he must be much more cunning. He thought he had made a reasonable start with the rebels. Simba clearly liked him. Well then, from now on he was going to be even more enthusiastic about everything. And Dinka? He had tried to be friendly with him, but the boy was moody. Best just be respectful, he decided.

He thought about Kito. He liked him a lot. How far did he trust him? Sam was sure Kito would not betray his real feelings about the rebels. How far could he rely on him?

He also remembered firing his rifle and the pleasure it had given him. He scowled up into the darkness and listened. It was starting to rain. The drops fell with a sharp crackle on to the tin roof. But he did not want to think about the gun any more. Besides, his father fired a gun. So it was not the gun's fault. The realisation pleased him. It gave him some sort of excuse. Now he was boxing clever and the thought pleased him. Soon after, he was fast asleep.

CHAPTER 16

For the next two days, they practised loading and unloading their rifles. They did it standing up at first, holding the gun vertically in front of them. It was hard work.

'Lots of weak little arms,' Captain Simba grumbled. 'Look at them shaking. Need to build those muscles. What say you, Dinka?'

The boy nodded.

When Simba was satisfied, they did the same thing again, only this time lying full length on the ground. This was much easier. Finally, Simba made them roll over on to their backs and hold the weapon above their faces.

'Need to know how to do this,' he explained. 'Specially if you're in low cover like short grass or maybe you hiding in a ditch, keeping your body safe out of sight.'

Despite everything, including Kito's sarcasm, Sam was developing a grudging respect for Simba. The man was a bully. No doubt about that. And a murderer. But things were somehow different in the rebel's world. Sam thought him not that much worse than some of the soldiers his father had told him about. During a break, he plucked up courage and approached Simba direct.

'Were you ever in the army, Boss?'

Captain Simba put his head on one side and studied him. 'Why you say that?'

'Because you know so much about it,' Sam replied simply.

Simba hesitated and smiled.

Sam was taken aback by the warmth of the man's reaction. It embarrassed him. 'Only, my father's a soldier,' Sam hurried on. 'He's a corporal—'

'And no friend of ours,' Dinka interrupted, joining them. He unslung his rifle. 'See that old crow by the mango tree?' he challenged. 'This is what we do to corporals in the army!'

He fired a long burst. The crow was tossed upwards in an explosion of black feathers.

'Join the others, Sam,' Captain Simba ordered.

* * *

In the afternoon, Simba taught them how to 'mamba' crawl. 'Lie flat. Like you was a snake,' he told them. 'Use your elbows and the sides of your knees to power yourself along. Keep your heads down. And your bottoms too!'

They took it in turns to drag themselves from tree to anthill or clump of grass while the others looked on and criticised. Sam thought the hardest bit was keeping the muzzle of his gun from digging into the ground.

'Look for cover all the time,' Captain Simba told them. 'A ditch, a tree trunk. Anything to hide your body from sight.'

Dinka yawned.

Captain Simba saw him. 'One day, it will save your life,' he shouted.

At the end of the second afternoon, Sam had raw patches on his elbows and legs, yet he felt more settled in himself than at any time since he had been taken from his village. Just before they were dismissed for the day, someone called out, 'Can we do more shooting? Shooting is great!'

'Lots more shooting,' Captain Simba told them, nodding happily. 'And if you all do well tomorrow, maybe you can join the rest of the Simba Boys next week. Maybe we can take you with us on an operation. Initiate you.'

After a good supper of goat stew and rice, Sam went to look for Kito. He found him sitting beside a wall, smoking.

'What's Simba been making you do?' Kito asked.

'Rifle drill and tactics,' Sam told him.

Kito sniggered. 'Playing at soldiers. That's what you really mean. Dinka told me all about it. Crawling on your bellies. Running and ducking down behind cover. Crazy!'

Sam frowned. 'But he's right!' he said indignantly. 'That's the proper way to learn combat techniques. My dad calls it "fire and movement".' He sat down opposite Kito. 'Half your mates fire at the enemy to keep their heads down. While they do that, the other half run forward to get closer to the enemy. That's how the army does it.'

Kito began to laugh. 'Sam, Sam,' he spluttered. 'You got so much to learn. Look! Captain Simba's Boys ain't exactly the Majungan Rifles. No matter how much Simba wants us to be.' And he laughed again.

'Can't you see your man Simba's just a toy soldier? We all know that. I do. So does Dinka. Don't you think Dada doesn't know it too? Simba's just another crazy.'

He reached forward and put a hand on Sam's shoulder.

'Listen, Sam, you want to know what happens for real? Remember, I've been there. I've seen it.' He shook his head and stared at the ground. 'When they go into action,' he said slowly, 'they're not rushing around looking for good places to fire from. Hell no! First thing to know is that they're out of their skulls on "brown-brown". That's gunpowder and cocaine, all mixed up. Then Colonel Dada the Merciful blesses them with holy water and says prayers over them. He tells them they safe from bullets and machetes and knives.'

'You mean, like the bullets are gonna bounce off them?' Sam jeered.

'Yep! You got it! So long as the children believe in Colonel Dada, they'll be safe. Nothing can touch them.'

Sam looked sceptical. 'And what happens when the children get killed or hurt bad? How does Dada talk his way out of that one?'

Kito smiled. 'Now that's the clever part. Dada tells them that those children that got killed or hurt lacked faith. They didn't believe in him enough. They weren't strong and true.'

'So it's all *their* fault?'

Kito nodded. 'That's about it.'

'It's like Colonel Dada thinks he's God or something,' Sam said bitterly.

'Colonel Dada *is* God,' Kito told him.

They took their usual walk around the compound. Sam felt depressed and didn't say much.

'What else did Simba tell you today?' asked Kito.

Sam told him. 'He's going to take us out on an operation soon. Going to "initiate" us.' He peered at Kito. 'What does "initiate" mean?'

Kito looked at him impatiently. 'What do you think it means?' And seeing Sam's expression, he scoffed, 'I thought you were smart? Isn't it obvious? OK. I'll tell you. Remember when you were circumcised?'

Sam's eyes widened. 'They can't do that again! Can they?'

Kito rubbed the side of his head in genuine exasperation. 'You crazy boy! Of course not. But that's an initiation thing too. It's something that makes you a full member of the family.'

'So what am I gonna have to do?'

Kito flicked the butt of his cigarette away. 'Kill somebody,' he said.

CHAPTER 17

'Sam! Got a job for you!' Captain Simba called.

'Yes, Boss!'

'One of the men soldiers on guard duty is gone sick,' Captain Simba told him. 'I want you to take his place. Tell the other men I sent you.'

Sam nodded enthusiastically.

'Take your gun with you and do just what they say.' He leaned towards the boy. 'This is a big honour, Sam. You the first of the new children to do guard.'

The guard post was on the track beside the main entrance to the camp. Three weeks ago, Simba had marched them up the hill towards it and the line of bleached skulls on either side. Sam remembered it well. When he got there, however, the two adult soldiers ignored him and went on talking quietly to each other.

Puzzled, he looked around and wondered what he should be doing.

The post consisted of a chest-high wall of sandbags. At the end nearest the track, the men had mounted a machine gun. Occasionally, one of them would peer over the sights and cover down the track. At the other end, the barricade had collapsed altogether. Sandbags lay tumbled randomly one on top of the other. As the sun climbed higher, the air in front of the post shimmered and swirled, and the red earth silently baked.

After a while, Sam became bored doing nothing. He laid his AK-47 on the ground and started to lift the sandbags back into place. They were heavy and he was soon pouring with sweat. The men watched him but said nothing. As he was heaving out the last one from a tangle of grass, a scorpion scuttled towards his hand, its sting raised high above its back. Sam jerked his hand away and leaped back. The scorpion made another short rush then disappeared back under the sandbag. Sam left it there.

He found the men looking at him with wide grins.

'Been meaning to do that for a long time,' one told him.

'Me too!' said the other. 'Just starting to think seriously about it.' He shook his head in mild admiration. 'You can come again anytime you want, boy.' And he laughed. He was about to say something else when the other man gave a warning grunt.

'Someone coming!' He clicked his tongue and pointed down the track.

Sam saw a cloud of dust coming along the track. A vehicle of some sort. One of the men passed him a pair of binoculars. Sam was thrilled. He had never used them before. He peered eagerly through the glasses. After a couple of seconds of searching, a white-painted vehicle surrounded by swirling clouds of red dust appeared.

'United Nations,' a guard told him. 'Friend of Colonel Dada.'

'How far away can you see with these?' Sam wanted to know.

The adult soldier shook his head and said nothing. Instead, he put out a large hand and took the binoculars back.

'You go tell Colonel Dada the UN is here,' he ordered.

Obediently, Sam picked up his AK-47 and ran towards the main compound. It was mid-morning and there were not many people around. A couple of men slept in the shade of a tree while the usual collection of child soldiers sat slumped against a wall. As he ran, he saw a line of women appear at the far end of the compound. They were carrying large bundles of washing on their heads and were coming from the direction of the river. Half a dozen child soldiers followed them in. These were the lookouts against lurking crocodiles.

At Colonel Dada's hut, Sam hesitated, suddenly feeling intimidated. Three wooden steps led up to a wide veranda. As he hesitated, Colonel Dada himself pushed through the swaying bead curtain.

'What is it, my son?' he demanded.

'Colonel, sir! The United Nations is coming.' And he indicated the sandbag emplacement, partly visible.

'How many vehicles?' Colonel Dada asked.

'One. Only one, sir! I think,' Sam added, now uncertain. 'Too much dust!'

The Colonel nodded and waved him away. He wore his usual priest's robe and carried an AK-47 over one shoulder. In addition, he had thrust a machete into a wide leather belt around his waist.

The white-painted Land Rover hooted three times and drove slowly into the compound. It pulled up beside Sam. The men inside let the dust settle then got out. There were two of them – the driver and a white man who walked around the front of the vehicle and sketched a salute.

Colonel Dada stood on top of the steps, beaming and holding out his hands in welcome. The white man called out something and they both laughed. As the man went up the steps, he missed his footing and stumbled, causing the canvas bag he was carrying to upend and a number of sheets of paper fell out. A swirl of wind caught them and sent them high into the air and across the compound.

Sam ran after them and spent the next few minutes chasing them down. The child soldiers watched him but did nothing to help. When he had gathered them all up, he ran back with the crumpled papers and handed them to the white man.

'Thank you!' the man said with a smile. 'And what's your name?'

Sam gulped with embarrassment and scratched the back of one leg with his big toe. 'Sam Mbali,' he said and for no particular reason added, 'My village is Tshombe.'

Perhaps it was his shyness talking. It was the first time he had ever spoken to a white man.

'Well, good luck, Sam!' the man said and smiled again. He shook hands with Colonel Dada on the veranda and they both went inside. The driver of the Land Rover gave him a small nod. Sam grinned back. He stood on tiptoe and peered into the back of the vehicle. He saw cooking pots and bedding and two large petrol cans all neatly stowed under the seats. There was a lot of room left.

He heard the driver curse and walked around to see what was wrong. The man had a cigar in his mouth and was flicking at a plastic lighter. He swore again and threw it away.

'I can get you a light,' Sam volunteered and hurried off to find Kito. They were back in a couple of minutes. The driver used the lighter and blew an appreciative cloud of smoke over both boys.

Sam pressed his nose to a side window and looked inside again. He wanted the driver to tell him to get in but was too shy to ask. The driver meanwhile put a hand in his shirt pocket and pulled out two packets of chewing gum. He gave them one each. Sam was thrilled. Then he remembered he was on guard duty and ran back to the sentry post.

'What you been doing?' one of the men grumbled. '*Una kazi mwingine*? Got another job?'

CHAPTER 18

That night, Sam lay on his back and stared into the darkness of the hut. The rats were very restless. He listened to their scamperings and wondered what it was they were always so busy doing. It had been the same at home, in the thatched roof of his family's hut. There were a lot of rats living up there. Sometimes a rat snake would climb up into the thatch and hunt them. When that happened, the rats would become frantic. Their panic-stricken squeaks would wake the dogs and set them off barking. His mother would reach for the broom she kept by the door and beat the dogs. Sam smiled at the memory.

He listened to the snores and troubled cries of the other twenty or so children in his hut and realised how much he hated them. Not Kito, of course, but every other one of Captain Simba's Boys. It wasn't their fault. None of them had volunteered to come here. They had all been kidnapped and their families destroyed. They were prisoners too. But most of them seemed to have accepted their lot and were content. Or perhaps it was the drugs they were given.

The other evening Kito had said, 'If you're a child in this country, how do you survive?' And Sam was slowly realising what he meant. If the grown-ups in your own village could not protect you, you became a child soldier yourself. If you wanted to eat, you joined God's Freedom Army. You'd probably be killed sometime soon but you'd certainly survive longer than just hiding in the forest, as so many adults did.

'In this life,' his father had often told him, 'you got to survive, Sam. Got to survive.' The last time he had said that, they had been sitting together on chairs outside their hut, waiting for supper. Tembo had a bottle of beer beside him. Every now and then, when there were no womenfolk around, he would hand it to Sam with a wink.

'You're born alone and you die alone,' he had said.

His mother had heard this and appeared holding a cooking ladle.

'Why you filling this boy's brain with these gloomy thoughts? You want to give him nightmares?

109

Besides, a boy has his mother there when he's born. So stop talking all this nonsense! Just drink your beer,' she added. 'And don't be getting that boy drunk, neither!'

Sam gave a little moan and hugged himself for comfort. Her voice was loud in his memory and her face so real, he put out his hands in the darkness to touch it. He loved her and all her funny little ways and knew he'd never see her again. He cried silently for a while. When all this was over, when he got out of this terrible dream, he'd go back to his village and try and find her grave.

Every night, he lived and relived that dreadful morning. It never got any easier to bear. The sound of gunfire and the screams, as they had led him away like a slave.

What had happened to his sisters? They must have been murdered there. Too young to be of any use. Left to die in the smoke and the flames by the rebels. By Captain Simba and Dinka and Colonel Dada. He hated them all so much.

Did his father even know about the attack on the village? Surely he must do by now. But where was he? Perhaps the Army knew all about Colonel Dada and were at this moment preparing to attack! He sat upright and listened. Dawn was not far off. A cockerel was already crowing. Soon, the wild birds would start to call. Another day would begin. And he'd have to be cheerful and keen so that no one here guessed the depth of his rage.

Sam had quickly learned that a wide grin was accepted at face value. His natural cheerfulness helped him disguise his real feelings. No one except Kito knew how far his hatred went. But as the sun rose and the compound began to come alive, he also realised that his life depended on keeping up the pretence. He must go on being 'Young Sam' as Captain Simba was now calling him. And that meant obeying the orders he was given. To refuse meant certain death. Like the girl in the forest. What choice did he have?

And what about the future? His own future? Did they really think he could kill other human beings? He wanted desperately to talk to Kito about it but something in his friend's own attitude stopped him. Kito had been there before him. And had survived. The boy was Sam's lifeline. He must respect Kito's reluctance to speak about these things and not demand too much sympathy.

He got to his feet and padded across to the door of the hut. Outside, the trees were etched black and unmoving against the sky. He heard women's voices and then someone began to sing. She sounded cheerful and almost happy. Sam ran towards the cookhouse. He wanted to share in it.

Later that morning, Dinka beckoned him over. Surprised, Sam went at once. These days, Dinka generally ignored him. 'Get our children together,' he ordered. 'Simba wants to talk to them.'

Soon, they were all squatting on the concrete floor of their hut, looking up at Captain Simba, who was striking his usual pose in front of them. Sam listened with a sinking heart. He guessed what was coming.

'I've got great news for every one of you,' Simba began. 'Tomorrow, at dawn, we go out on a big mission.' He put a hand on his pistol holster and stared around in triumph.

'We're going to have a good time!' He waited for a moment then frowned. 'I said, we're going to have a GOOD TIME!' And he stood, hands on hips, glaring at them.

A ragged cheer went up.

'We're going to save souls and bring them back here to live with us.' There was another cheer, this time louder than the first.

Captain Simba looked over at Sam and his grin faded.

'What's wrong with you, young Sam? You don't look happy no more.'

Sam gave a start and flashed the man his widest smile. 'I am, sir! Oh yes I am!' he exclaimed and nodded vigorously. He caught Dinka's eye and looked quickly away. *Too* quickly, he thought. That might have been a mistake. Dinka was smart. And watchful. He'd better take a lot more care in the future.

Captain Simba continued. 'We're going to a village twenty kilometres away. We've got a truck to take us there.' The children cheered again, this time with genuine enthusiasm. He smiled at them. 'Here is my plan. The truck will drop us off an hour's march from the village. I will lead the column. Dinka and Sam will be at the rear to keep the children all together. You hear?'

Dinka and Sam nodded.

'When we get to the village,' Simba went on, 'we form up in one line like I've taught you.' He leaned towards them. 'We're going to surprise them, so we move in real quiet-like. Each of you then wait by a hut. When I fire into the air, you get the people in there out. Remember, only the children will be saved. No one else. Everyone understand?'

They all seemed to.

'One last thing.' He waved a warning finger at

them. 'Colonel Dada will be there to see us leave. Make sure you behave like soldiers. Stand tall. Be proud. Like all Captain Simba's Boys!'

CHAPTER 19

Dawn. A cool breeze blew scurries of sand across the compound. A battered-looking truck waited in the middle, its engine running. In front of it, the door of a new four-by-four opened and Captain Simba slid out. He patted its side admiringly then bent to check his appearance in the wing mirror. He adjusted the brown beret he often wore, and stamped his feet hard so that the creases in his combat kit looked sharper. Then he marched towards them.

'Get into two ranks!' Dinka yelled. 'Cigarettes out!'

One of the very young child soldiers turned away and started to retch. 'Too much chicken stew last night.' Dinka scowled. 'Greedy little pig!'

Sam thought it more likely to be the hash the child had been smoking but said nothing. He too was feeling wobbly. His head was muzzy and the only place he wanted to be was stretched out on his sleeping mat. All Captain Simba's children had been given an issue of hashish an hour ago. Dinka had told them it would make them as brave as lions and everyone believed him. Sam had no idea how true it was, but Captain Simba, for one, was convinced.

'It's like a secret weapon,' he had told Sam the evening before. 'Like rocket fuel. It makes every one of the children as strong as men. That's why you must have it, Sam. Set a good example. But if you throw up over my boots, I'll shoot you!' And he had gone away laughing. Sam had now smoked three joints. Two of them this morning.

After the initial revulsion, the only effect they had had on him was to make him feel sleepy and very thirsty. The other children, for their part, thought it wonderful. Most of them smoked it anyway, whenever they could. Dinka mixed it with frequent swigs of rum from the metal water bottle he carried at his waist.

Sam watched Captain Simba coming towards them. He tried to stop himself swaying. He felt sick and his eyes kept blurring. He blinked furiously and gripped the sling of his AK-47 simply for something to hang on to. There were two full bandoliers of ammunition

116

draped across his shoulders. They felt heavy and cold against his ragged T-shirt. They had all been promised proper combat kit weeks ago but this had still not arrived. Rumours were flying around the compound that a rival band of children under the command of General Ubique had moved into the nearby area and had ambushed the lorry carrying the uniforms.

Sam's thoughts were interrupted by Captain Simba's shouted order to stand to attention. From the corner of his eye, he saw the tall figure of Colonel Dada approaching. He was carrying his cross, holding it high in front of him. This time, a dead snake had been pinned to it. His rifle was on his shoulder and he wore the usual row of medals across his chest.

Captain Simba saluted smartly and bent his head as the Colonel blessed him. Colonel Dada put a long hand on Simba's shoulder then slapped him gently on both cheeks. The boy next to Sam giggled nervously. Colonel Dada turned and stared at the children. He raised the cross and began to chant. Sam dropped his gaze, unwilling to meet the Colonel's. The chant went on for several minutes. There was something hypnotic about it. When at last it stopped, Colonel Dada spoke to them.

'This is the first time you go to do God's work. I have been praying for you.'

'Alleluja!' several of the children called out. Sam was surprised by that.

Colonel Dada's voice rose. 'You need not be afraid, any of you. If you truly believe, then no bullets will hit you. No knives will cut you. No one will harm a hair on your head. If you are a true believer, God will keep you safe. This I, Colonel Dada the Merciful, swear to you!'

A sigh of reassurance rippled through the children. Sam watched their shoulders straighten and saw the grins they exchanged with one another. There was no doubt about it; Dada had lifted a great deal of worry and fear from them. Sam stared at the Colonel, who was now shaking hands with Captain Simba. Despite himself, he wondered if the man did not after all possess magical powers. He was so calm, so certain. Whether he did or did not, Sam *wanted* him to have them. He needed to know that he too would be safe.

'Go well, my sons,' Colonel Dada called and stood to one side watching, while Captain Simba marched the children towards the transport. The truck driver helped them clamber on board then swung up the tailboard with a bang and bolted it.

'Shut up the lot of you!' Dinka shouted once they were all in. 'You're like a bunch of monkeys!'

Sam didn't mind. He felt reassured and couldn't help grinning at the others and nodding when they smiled back. For the first time since he had been here, he felt some sort of human kinship with them. Not just with the children from his own village, but with the other sad little strangers here as well. Sam's mood lasted until the truck eventually stopped to let them off. Then, reality returned. Surrounded by thorn bushes and biting flies, they formed up in a small column and followed Captain Simba into the unknown.

The sun blazed down and they were hot and bad-tempered by the time they reached the outskirts of the village. Here they stopped and took cover. Captain Simba waved Dinka and Sam to come forward and join him.

'There's something wrong,' he whispered, as they slid in alongside him. He pointed to where the village lay, fifty metres beyond the line of scrub to their front. 'Listen! There's no noise.'

He was right, Sam thought. Villages were noisy places. People calling to one another. Babies crying. Dogs barking. But here, there was none of that. Just a thick blanket of silence. He looked at the sky and saw a crowd of vultures circling. There was always at least one of them waiting over every village but here Sam counted thirteen. He nudged Captain Simba and pointed.

Simba's eyes widened. He thought for a moment. 'You stay and take charge,' he told Dinka. 'Me and Sam will have a look around. Be ready to give us covering fire if I shout. You remember what that is? I tried to teach you, remember?' And he gave Dinka a nasty look. 'Come on, Sam. Safety catch off!'

They bent double and went forward carefully. Through the screen of grass and thin bushes, Sam saw the tops of thatched roofs appear. The next moment, the brown sides of the huts themselves became visible. They looked so familiar.

Sam stared at them. They were like home. Like his own hut. He could almost imagine his mother coming out of one of them. Or his sisters. He had an overwhelming desire to get closer, to see who was there.

He pushed past Simba, ignoring the man's startled exclamation. There was a great iron band tightening across his brow. He thought he could hear his skull cracking. He began to run.

Now he was out in the open, his finger lying on alongside the trigger. The village lay in front of him. His stomach heaved. He faltered as the bile came up and splashed into the back of his mouth. It burned his nostrils and dripped down on to his chest. A fly settled on his lip. He spat bile at it, turned his head away and saw a dead man lying in the entrance of a hut.

He was old and lay on his back, mouth wide open and drawn back over long, stained teeth. Flies as big as bumble bees swarmed over his smashed chest. There were flies everywhere, buzzing in a demented frenzy. A rat appeared. It stood on its hind legs beside the body, then jumped up and dipped its snout inside.

This was what it had been like in his village. And now it was happening again. All around him. Sam could see it. Smell it. Something like an angry hornet brushed past his head. He felt his ear seized in a red hot vice. He yelled in pain and stared in disbelief at the blood that ran down the front of his shirt. He saw movement in front of him. A stream of bullets raced across the ground towards him. He threw himself to one side and heard the crack-crack as they went past. There were other children there. In uniform. Trying to kill him as they had so brutally killed these poor villagers.

What little reason Sam had left snapped. He ran forward, shouting and hurling insults at the men and boys who had done this. He was ducking and bending and firing whenever he saw a target. These were the people who had killed his own family.

Twenty metres away, three child soldiers broke cover and fled from a hut. Without breaking step, Sam changed his magazine for a full one and went after them. The nearest one saw Sam, turned and began shooting. It was a brave thing to do but Sam never faltered. He held the rifle in against his side and fired. The child fell backwards, throwing out his arms as he did so. His AK-47 landed on the ground beside his head. It was stuck on automatic and went on firing blindly at ankle height. Sam leaped over him and took aim at the other two. He saw his bullets hitting home and a boy pitching forward. Then the magazine was empty.

This time, he fumbled the reload. He dropped the full magazine in the dust and, for a couple of seconds, was at anyone's mercy. By the time he had finished, the third soldier had disappeared. Sam's body sagged. He was heavy with sweat and his legs trembled uncontrollably. His mind was drained of emotion.

He spotted Simba and ran wearily towards him. Captain Simba was crouching behind the village well. He stuck out a hand and pulled Sam down beside him.

'Boy!' he said. 'That was some rocket fuel you was on!' And he laughed.

'Who are these other children?' Sam gasped.

Captain Simba shook his head. 'Ubique's boys?

Don't know. Don't care. They all gonna die.'

A group of enemy children was now heading towards them. Bullets were starting to whip overhead and thud into the bricks on the other side of the well. Sam could feel the shockwaves from where he lay. He looked anxiously at Simba. If they didn't make a run for the trees in the next few seconds, the advancing enemy children would catch them, right out in the open. They'd be the easiest of targets. 'I've not got much ammo left,' he warned.

Simba funnelled his hands and shouted, 'DINKA! FIRE!'

Sam thought he heard the boy shouting back but then everything was drowned by the yells of the advancing enemy. They hurried forward, bunching together in an untidy scrum and all heading for the well. Sam could hear Simba shouting at the top of his voice. He had a sudden vision of Dinka's sneering face and, for the first time that morning, Sam was really frightened.

Fifty metres away, the enemy children broke into a shambling run. Sam thought there must have been thirty of them, at least. From the bottom of the brickwork, he took aim. He tried to fire well-aimed shots, as Captain Simba had taught them. But it wasn't as easy out here. Not when you were doing it for real.

Meanwhile, the enemy children were whooping with excitement and urging each other on. Most were firing from the hip. Some seemed content to shoot high into the air and go on screaming.

'Dinka!' Captain Simba screamed. Sam heard the desperation in his voice as the man struggled up into a kneeling position. For a split second, Sam thought he was going to make a run for it.

There was a sudden loud volley of gunfire and the oncoming children wavered. There were bodies falling and rolling on the ground. The rest hesitated then came on. A row of bullets smacked into the bricks just above Sam's head and he was covered in a cloud of red-hot fragments.

Another volley from the scrub and more boys were falling. The children wavered and turned uncertainly towards this unseen enemy. Half a dozen of them still ran towards the well.

'They think their magic is strong!' Simba shouted at Sam. He snapped on a fresh magazine and blazed away at them.

There were loud yells from the scrub and Captain Simba's Boys charged into the open.

'Good soldiers! Good soldiers!' Simba roared. The enemy children were in full retreat now. Dinka and the others were stooping over bodies and pulling away their weapons. There were short bursts of fire as the wounded were dealt with. Tears were running down Captain Simba's cheeks. 'God's own boys!' he cried, pinching his nose in emotion.

He hugged Dinka then blew his nose, loudly. 'Back to the truck!' he ordered. 'Before they come again.'

'What about our wounded?' Sam asked. 'The bad ones?'

'Dinka knows what to do,' Captain Simba said. 'Only be quick about it, Dinka. Hear me?'

He led them off at a run back into the scrub. Behind them, Sam heard a couple of single shots. Soon, Dinka caught up with him. Together, the two boys jogged along and brought up the rear. Dinka carried three extra AK-47s but didn't seem to notice. He was in a world of his own and ignored Sam.

The ground was strewn with large boulders. As he ran past one, Sam saw movement and looked. There was a boy huddled against the rock. He was in uniform and holding a rifle. Sam yelled and brought his own gun up. The other boy's eyes rolled and he dropped to his knees. His AK-47 fell to the ground. Sam stared at him and cautiously advanced. He stooped and picked up the weapon.

The boy started to moan. His cries grew louder. He began to sway backwards and forwards, blubbering for his mother. Dinka came to see what was happening and promptly kicked the boy in the chest. The boy lay on his side and covered his face with both hands.

'Deserter,' Dinka said. 'Running away. Do you want his uniform?'

They stared at him. Dinka wrinkled his nose. 'He's messed himself.'

'What do we do with him?' Sam asked.

Dinka shrugged. 'He's your prisoner. Up to you. Me? I'd shoot him.' He turned away and jogged after the others.

The boy on the ground had understood. He flung his hands out on either side of his body and began banging his forehead on the ground. 'Please, sir! Please, sir!'

Sam looked at him. The boy was at his mercy. He stared at his bobbing head. The nape of his neck was as smooth as a baby's. He couldn't have been much more than seven years old. He picked up the boy's rifle. It seemed to weigh a ton. He cocked it. The boy squealed like a frightened little pig.

Sam fired a short burst high into the air. Then he slung the gun over his shoulder and ran for it. He had done terrible things that day. Perhaps God would forgive him for some of them now . . .

'All done?' Dinka asked when he caught up.

Sam nodded.

'Good!' Dinka said. 'Like your ear. Looks great!'

CHAPTER 20

Captain Simba gave a shout and pointed down the track.

'There's the truck! Come on! Hurry!'

It was the best thing Sam had seen in months. The driver appeared from behind a bush and gave them a cheery wave. He walked across to the vehicle and pulled himself up into the cab. The engine came to life unenthusiastically, pouring out thick black exhaust. Sam forced himself to run the last few metres then sagged against a back wheel in pure relief. He had never been so exhausted before. Not even when they had first been kidnapped and were walking through the forest. His head was pounding and every muscle in his body felt tender. The others, grouped around, clearly felt the same.

Only Captain Simba showed any animation. He took a quick head count, then shouted, 'In the truck! All of you! Now!'

While the boys were clambering on board, he ran back some of the way and stood looking down the track. A boy appeared, limping badly. Sam saw Simba put his hands to his mouth.

'You want to be ambushed? Come on! Hurry!'

The boy staggered and almost fell, then came slowly on again.

By now, Captain Simba was almost dancing with impatience. Abruptly, he ran towards the boy, seized him around the waist and carried him back to the truck. He bundled him up over the tailboard where willing hands dragged him inside. The boy's screams followed Simba as he rushed towards his own four-by-four.

Meanwhile, in the truck, everyone wanted to touch Sam's wounded ear. It was soon bleeding again.

'That's very powerful magic!' someone said, squeezing down on the floor beside him. 'That bullet should have killed you. Now everyone will stick as close to you as possible.'

The truck driver clashed the gears and the vehicle shook violently. It took off with a sudden lurch that sent them all sprawling. Sam fought his way upright and hung on to the side of the vehicle. Dust billowed in, so that for the first few minutes no one could see anything. The truck hit a pothole with a spine-bruising crash and then another. Sam fumbled for his water bottle and found it empty. There was nothing he could do about it. Nothing he could do about anything.

For no reason in particular, he remembered the priest who often came to his village. Father Benoit was a popular visitor. He was a tall man who came from the coast. He used to show them photographs of his family's fishing boat. It had a large red eye painted on either side of its bows. Sam also remembered that the priest had once told them that Man was God's greatest creation. But now, Sam knew the priest had been wrong. Squashed in the back of Colonel Dada's truck like this, Sam and all the other children were as important as a swarm of flies.

He closed his eyes and listened to the sound of the engine straining and the driver's curses. He thought of the flies crawling over the bodies back in that village. That was how his mother must have looked. Her friendly brown eyes staring unblinking at the sky while flies fed greedily on her tears.

He made a grab for the tailboard and threw up over it. Afterwards, he went to sleep.

* * *

There was trouble brewing when they got back. As the lorry drove into the compound, its steering gear failed and it almost rammed the steps leading up to Colonel Dada's building. His escort came out to watch, their fingers on triggers.

Captain Simba banged on the vehicle's side and ordered everyone off.

'Form up as usual,' he ordered and went to help the injured boy and lay him on the ground. It was obvious now that his leg was broken. The boy lay there moaning. His cries grew louder.

Colonel Dada came down the steps and scowled at the boy. He walked straight past him and stood beside Captain Simba. There, he began to count the boys on parade. He took a step closer and counted again. When he had finished, he flung himself around.

'How many boys went with you?'

Captain Simba saluted. Dust drifted down from his beret.

'Twenty-seven, Colonel.'

Dada glared at him. 'And you bring back twenty-two! Where are the missing five?'

Captain Simba blinked, taken aback by the question.

'There was fighting,' he explained. 'Enemy forces were in the village. We drove them away.'

'How many new recruits have you brought back?'

Simba shook his head. 'None! The village children were already taken by the enemy.'

Sam watched, fascinated. He almost felt sorry for Captain Simba. And he had never seen the man look so unsure of himself.

'My boys fought well,' Simba protested. 'You would have been proud of them.'

Colonel Dada stood unmoving but his voice grew strangely higher pitched. 'But I told you to bring back new boys. Not to leave five of my own behind!'

He tore the rifle from his shoulder and fired into a nearby tree. Twigs and small branches fell.

'What happened to my five boys?' he shouted.

Simba gulped, visibly.

'Two dead and three wounded, Colonel, sir!'

Dada's face contorted. 'Three wounded? You left behind three wounded to be tortured? Or worse, to join that monster Ubique?'

Dinka stepped forward and shouted at the top of his voice. 'I shot all the wounded, Colonel, sir. Just like you told me.'

Colonel Dada turned on him like an angry snake. 'Then who's that boy lying on the ground there?' he spat. 'Can't you count?'

He brushed past Captain Simba and almost ran towards the boy.

'I've no use for wounded boys,' he screamed. 'This is not a hospital. They must learn to take their medicine!'

And he fired, raking the boy from head to foot.

When it was over, he reloaded and went up the stairs. He did not look back.

CHAPTER 21

Mr Schratte's secretary Martine was a motherly-looking woman of middle age. She was small, rosy-cheeked and smelled faintly of lavender water. She had a ready smile and an easy-going manner. Visitors who didn't know her thought of her as 'very pleasant'. Her eyes, though, were shrewd and missed nothing. She had been with Mr Schratte for over twenty years. Her father had been with him in the Congo, in the old days. He had met his death in an ambush there.

She knew almost as much about Mr Schratte's business affairs as he did. Her memory for faces and events was astonishing.

'She knows where the bodies are buried,' Mr Schratte often joked when introducing her to prospective business clients. 'Not surprising, seeing as she helped dig most of their graves,' had been the bitter response from someone who had once fallen foul of her.

When the telephone rang that evening, she guessed it was Jean Morrell. She had not yet decided whether she trusted him or not. She was already doing some careful checking of her own.

'Mr Morrell for you,' she said to Schratte. 'On line two.'

'Record it for me, Martine,' he told her. 'We need to get all this down on tape.'

He waited a moment, then, 'So where are you now, Jean?' Mr Schratte asked.

'Back in the field. I've made contact with our client.'

There was a pause. 'And how is he?'

'Very keen to meet you and discuss final details. He's hot to trot, as they say.'

Mr Schratte sat forward in his chair. 'Good.'

'He wants to discuss the financial arrangements with you, personally. He's looking for a substantial payment in advance. To show good faith. That sort of thing.' Jean Morrell sounded hopeful.

Mr Schratte grunted and made doodles on a notepad. 'Listen, Jean,' he replied. 'You say he's keen to meet me. Well, that's nothing to how I feel about him. I need to check things out myself. I've some heavy hitters at my end, very interested in this project. But they're the sort of people who don't like anything going wrong. Or not being properly thought through, if you know what I mean.'

Jean Morrell said, 'There's a flight from Paris out to Douceville in two days' time. I can charter something small and then fly you up here, if you like. The client will meet us and provide a bodyguard. What do you think?'

'I'll want to pick up my own muscle at Douceville,' Mr Schratte insisted.

'No problem. I'll get on with it. So you'll come?'

Mr Schratte nodded. 'I'll be there.'

He looked up. Martine stood in the doorway. 'Which passport do you want to use?' she asked.

CHAPTER 22

The aircraft came in low over a line of acacia trees, its wings see-sawing in the fierce thermals close to the ground. It was a small, propeller-driven machine that had once been the apple of some company chairman's eye. Now, its paintwork had long since faded and its engine sounded irritable.

It hit the ground with a bang and, for a moment, Mr Schratte thought the undercarriage had collapsed. He grabbed the seat in front and braced himself. Then they were bumping and swaying over the ground to a growing chorus of groans and crackles from the ancient airframe.

Airstrips I have known, he thought, staring at the piece of canvas that separated the pilot from his three passengers. He snatched a glance at Jean Morrell, sitting across the narrow gangway. His eyes were closed. Perhaps he was praying? Mr Schratte shrugged. Just so long as he wasn't sick. The pilot would dine out on that sort of story for weeks afterwards. And that was the last thing Mr Schratte wanted.

The engine gave a final bellow as the plane slewed around. Its wingtip missed a derelict-looking shed by not much more than a metre. Mr Schratte's knuckles whitened. He couldn't decide whether the pilot was a total incompetent who'd be better off driving a hearse or a first-class bush flyer. Morrell had hired him and presumably checked him out. At least, he hoped so.

'Bit hairy, that,' Morrell exclaimed, puffing out his cheeks in relief.

Mr Schratte said nothing. There was no point. Instead, he unclipped his frayed seat-belt and sat still in order to regain his composure. The pilot appeared. He was a big, beefy man with a red face.

'Sorry about that, gents!' he called genially. 'Now you know why this *isn't* the world's favourite airline!' And he chuckled.

South African, Mr Schratte decided. *Probably left at the end of the apartheid era, when Mandela and black Africans came to power.*

The pilot was thrusting the main door open. It swung back and a wave of hot, damp air filled the cabin. Mr Schratte smiled. Africa! It had a smell like no other part of the world. Perspiration was already gathering on his face and even in here the sound of grasshoppers was loud and shrill. He was back, and it felt good. Very good.

The shed was made of sheets of corrugated iron. Several of them were missing and tall weeds sprouted up through the gaps. The termites had eaten away most of the wooden frame so that the shed leaned heavily to one side. Mr Schratte wondered why it had been built here in the first place. And by whom?

'This is the place,' Morrell told him. 'I recognise it, all right.' He shaded his eyes and looked around. 'I wonder how long they'll be.'

Mr Schratte shrugged. 'They'll have heard us. They'll be along soon enough.'

His bodyguard walked purposefully towards the end of the hut and, turning his back on them, opened his fly.

'So, I wait here till you guys return?' the pilot asked.

Jean Morrell nodded. 'Right! I've no idea how long we'll be. Six hours? Maybe more?'

The pilot rubbed his jaw. 'So long as a rhino or a herd of elephants don't take a fancy to us, we'll be here.'

'They've all been poached years ago—' Mr Schratte

started to tell him when Morrell touched his shoulder.

'Look!' He pointed. 'It's them.'

A distant dust cloud was growing bigger. Soon they could make out two four-by-four vehicles bouncing over the ground towards them. They came to a halt close to the aircraft. The pilot swore fluently as his plane disappeared behind a dense cloud of dust. Coughing and choking, the others ran to one side to avoid the worst of it.

A large man in military uniform emerged from the dust and walked briskly towards them. He wore a necklace of lions' claws. Behind him, they could now see that the four-by-fours were packed with child soldiers armed with AK-47s and rocket launchers.

Jean Morrell stepped forward and held out his hand. 'I'm Jean Morrell,' he said politely. 'And this is Jack Schratte. Good to meet you.'

The man saluted smartly. 'I'm Captain Simba, Colonel Dada's right hand man. I've come to take you to him.' He shook hands with the two Europeans and then for the first time noticed Mr Schratte's bodyguard. He frowned.

'This man must stay here. For his own safety.'

Mr Schratte winked at the bodyguard. 'I'll be fine, Pauli. You wait here and keep an eye on the plane for me.'

Captain Simba stalked towards the vehicles. 'If you don't mind travelling with my men,' he indicated the back of the nearest four-by-four, 'we've made you comfortable seats.'

The child soldiers watched in silence as the two Belgians climbed in. They studied the newcomers' shoes and the watches they wore. Most of them refused to make eye contact. Except for one boy. He grinned cheerfully at Jean Morrell while the vehicle crashed and banged along a rutted track. Rather embarrassed, Jean Morrell smiled back at the lop-sided figure with only half an ear. The boy leaned towards him.

'You remember me, sir?' he shouted.

Jean Morrell strained his memory. Yes he did! And as he did so, the name popped out. 'Sam!' he said. And saw the boy's face beam with pleasure. 'Sam Mbali? From . . .'

'Tshombe, sir! My father is a corporal in the army.'

The boy's companions broke into laughter and started chattering away to one another.

Poor little guy, Morrell thought and racked his brains to think of something else to say. 'What regiment is your dad in?'

This was clearly a good question. The boy laughed and nodded enthusiastically. 'The Majunga Rifles, sir! They call him Corporal Tembo.'

'And Tembo means "elephant". Am I right?' Morrell asked.

A bigger boy leaned over and smacked the side of Sam's head. Sam aimed a punch back. An AK-47 clattered on to the metal floor of the Land Rover. The vehicle braked and Captain Simba erupted out of the cab and restored order.

'Who's the boy?' Mr Schratte asked, when they were moving again.

'Just some boy or other,' Morrell told him. 'I met him at Dada's headquarters.'

Mr Schratte nudged him. 'Always call people here by their titles, Jean. They get sensitive about that sort of thing.'

'*Colonel* Dada's headquarters,' Morrell said quickly.

Half an hour later, they began to run along the side of a slow-moving river. 'That's the Baruba. Our river. Not far now,' announced Captain Simba.

Colonel Dada was waiting for them. His ceremonial throne had been brought from the camp down to the riverbank and placed under the shade of a palm tree. He was dressed in his usual robes.

'Oh my God!' breathed Mr Schratte. 'Another bloody madman.'

There were handshakes all around and much back-slapping between Jean Morrell and the Colonel. The

Colonel spread his arms wide and prayed for the success of the 'project', as he called it. A pot of coffee was produced and a large plate full of dates and wild fruits.

'That reminds me,' said Mr Schratte, smiling at Colonel Dada. 'I have a small present for you. I met the Bishop of Knocke recently and he remembered you. He suggested you might find a use for this.'

He opened his briefcase and brought out a slim, expensively-wrapped gift. Jean Morrell gave him a sideways glance. Colonel Dada's long fingers eagerly ripped open the packaging. He gave a grunt of pleasure and took out a solid gold fountain pen. He pulled the top off and admired it from all angles.

'It has your name on one side,' Mr Schratte told him. 'May I show you?'

'And how is the Bishop these days?' Colonel Dada wanted to know. 'I was with him for a few months at a seminary many years ago. Then my work brought me back here.'

'I know,' Mr Schratte told him. 'And he sends you his blessing.'

'And you must give him mine.'

Jean Morrell blinked. It was true what they said. Mr Schratte knew everything there was to know about doing business here. He smiled at the Colonel.

They took Mr Schratte along the riverbank to the place where Jean Morrell had found the gold.

'My colleague has given you a copy of the report from our gold experts in Antwerp?' Mr Schratte asked.

Colonel Dada nodded. 'Yes! It was good! Now let's talk business. You're going to pay me fifty thousand dollars a year to run the diggings for you. And half of the monthly take each month. You agree?'

Mr Schratte looked at him. 'Just tell me how and where you want the money paid.'

'Ten thousand immediately to my bank here in Majunga. The rest to an account with the Chartered Bank of Geneva. Head office.' He dug inside his robes and pulled out a folded piece of paper. 'Here are my account details. As soon as I have confirmation that the money has arrived, I start work for you on the terms we have already agreed.'

'And my representative will arrive twenty-four hours later to assist your own middlemen with the accounting procedures,' Mr Schratte confirmed.

'Colonel Dada, you'll provide the security and discipline—' Jean Morrell began to say.

'And build the miners a camp and a cookhouse and bring in their food and drink, and read them a bedtime story . . . Yes! Yes! Yes!' Colonel Dada cried impatiently. 'I *have* done this before!'

'I've not worked with child soldiers before,' Mr Schratte said conversationally, to cover an awkward silence. 'Tell me, Colonel. Are they as good as people say?'

Dada's scowl disappeared as if by magic. 'They're God's gift to the free world,' he said and put back his head and laughed. Then he held up his hand and began ticking off points on his fingers.

'They don't need paying. They do what they're told. They're brave and, most of all, they're easily replaced.' He broke into peals of laughter, stopping eventually to blow his nose on a large white handkerchief. He shook his head at them and smiled broadly.

'In short, my friends, they're worth their weight in gold!' And he started laughing again.

Later that night at Bukavu Airport and after one glass of champagne too many, Jean Morrell asked a question that had been bothering him all afternoon.

'Jack? Why are we letting Dada cream off fifty per cent of the monthly takings. I mean, isn't that a little too generous?'

Mr Schratte swirled the contents of his glass around and smiled.

'It's what I call "seed money",' he said. And seeing

the younger man's puzzled expression, he went on, 'We need Colonel Dada and his ghastly crew to do the dirty work and to get the place up and running. That's why I'm prepared to be so generous. I need him to be there.

'However,' he paused and looked over his shoulder then dropped his voice, 'when I judge the time is right, I'll go and see friends of mine in the Majungan government and offer it to them, at a more commercial rate. Which means, of course, a better one for us.'

Morrell stared at him.

'If the Majungan government can get their act together and, more importantly, their army in position, then we can tempt them with an irresistible deal. They'll be able to destroy Dada *and* get a healthy stake in a working, profitable gold mine, at one stroke.'

'A double whammy!' Morrell whistled. 'And we'll get a lot more for ourselves.'

Mr Schratte smiled at him. 'They've been after Dada for a long time. He's been a big thorn in their side, politically. Cost them a lot of foreign investment. A lot of back-handers too. They've tried very hard to catch him but he's been elusive. They've never got near him. Now, with this goldmine, he's suddenly tied down to one place.

'Between you and me, Jean,' he added confidentially,

'I much prefer to work with governments. They're more long lasting and know the rules. Besides, I'm just about ready to sell the Majungans a whole lot of nice new shiny armoured cars.'

Jean Morrell laughed.

'Come on!' Mr Schratte told him. 'That's my flight they're announcing. Time for me to go!'

CHAPTER 23

Two days later, in the early afternoon, Jean Morrell parked his white UN Land Rover outside the best hotel in the capital, Douceville. He had decided it was time he took an afternoon off work. Heaven knows, he deserved it. He dismissed his driver and drove himself through the imposing wrought-iron gates into the perfectly manicured grounds of the hotel. He parked with a flourish and sauntered happily towards the great glass front doors.

He was in a very good mood. He was enjoying working for the UN. What he did was interesting and he was very much his own master. He met a wide variety of people. Some of them he was able to help, and this gave him a satisfaction he had never known before. But above all was the knowledge that, thanks to his working relationship with Jack Schratte, he was going to be a very rich man, very very soon.

The Hotel Splendide was an important meeting place for the country's elite. Here, they could rub shoulders with international business people, journalists and senior executives from many of the world's leading aid organisations. There was another clientele too, who used the place. A floating population who preferred to keep out of the limelight. These were people who could 'fix' things. Importers and exporters of everything from sacks of rice to ivory tusks. Hardbitten men who came and went and of whom no one asked too many questions.

Jean Morrell pushed through the swing doors of the main bar and strode through the discreet gloom. Philipe, the barman, greeted him with a professional smile.

'The usual, Mr Morrell?'

Jean Morrell nodded. He pulled up a tall bar stool and eagerly waited for his brandy sour.

'Quiet today,' he remarked to the world at large.

Philipe agreed. 'They'll be in later. After the afternoon siesta.' He chuckled. 'And then, we'll never get rid of them.'

The only other person at the bar was a good-looking young African in a well-cut jacket and chino trousers. He nodded at Morrell.

'Philipe's right. I was here last night. You should have seen them.'

'Oh I know, I know,' Jean Morrell told him. 'That's when I normally come. Isn't that so, Philipe?'

The barman flicked a tea towel at a passing fly. 'You right there, Mr Morrell. Every two weeks, you come. Regular as clockwork.'

The telephone at the end of the bar began to ring. Philipe went to answer it. When he had finished he made a face and looked at his two customers. 'The general manager needs me to do something. I may be five minutes. You gentlemen like another one till I get back?'

'Sure, why not,' cried Morrell. He looked towards the younger man. 'What'll you have?'

The man smiled. 'Just a beer, please. Thank you!'

They drank in silence for a while. Then Jean Morrell asked, 'Work for the government?'

The younger man nodded. 'Yes. But not here. Not in Douceville. I'm stationed in Eastern Province, near Kuwanda.'

Morrell considered. 'That's a long way from here.'

'Don't I know it. It's taken me two whole days to get here.' Then he added by way of explanation, 'I'm on leave from the army.'

Morrell nodded to himself. 'Army, eh? I'm with the

150

UN, for my sins.' He thrust out his hand. 'Jean Morrell.'

The young man took it. 'Joshua Mbote. Captain,' he said shyly.

Jean Morrell smiled at him. 'Which regiment?'

'The Majungan Rifles.'

Philipe reappeared behind the bar. He rubbed his hands in mock satisfaction and grinned at them. 'All done. Easy.'

Jean Morrell looked at his watch.

'Have you time for a return drink?' the young captain asked.

Morrell considered. Then nodded. 'Just the one.'

They toasted each other. 'Were you ever in the army?' Captain Mbote asked.

Jean Morrell grinned. 'No. My dad was. A long time ago. But I don't think you'd want to hear too much about him or his unit. Or what they did.'

Seeing Captain Mbote frown, Morrell said, 'Funny, you being in the Rifles.'

Looking even more puzzled, Mbote asked, 'Why?'

'Well,' Jean Morrell paused. 'I met someone recently who was . . .' he hesitated. 'That is, he said his father was in the Rifles. As far as I can remember.'

'I don't follow you.'

Morrell scratched his head. 'There was this boy. He

151

said his name was Sam. His father was a corporal in the Rifles. I don't suppose that's of any interest to you,' he ended, lamely.

Captain Mbote's face was expressionless. 'Where did you meet this child?'

'Oh. A long way from here. Up by the Baruba River. I've forgotten exactly where. I think he was with Colonel Dada's people.' He looked at his watch and gave a start. 'Grief. That the time? I really must run.' He put out his hand. 'Good luck, Captain. Enjoy your leave. Bye, Philipe.'

After he had gone, Captain Mbote took out a new banknote and casually slid it towards the barman. 'Tell me,' he said. 'Who exactly was that?'

Later, he tried to telephone his regiment in Kuwanda but the line was dead. There was nothing unusual about that. Oh well, he'd be reporting back at the end of the week. He could tell the adjutant about it then, of course. But it was an extraordinary coincidence. The boy's name. And what was this UN man doing with Dada's bunch of thugs? He thought for a while longer and then decided he'd give his brother-in-law, the Minister, a call.

CHAPTER 24

'The Minister is free now, Captain,' said the aide, opening the door for Joshua Mbote.

The Captain had never been in his brother-in-law's office before. It was on the fifth floor of the most modern building in Douceville. Its location reflected the importance of the ministry within the Majungan government. The Minister himself was in shirtsleeves and came from behind a large desk to shake hands. He waved Mbote to a comfortable chair. 'Coffee? Tea? Something stronger?'

Captain Mbote smiled and shook his head. 'No thank you, sir.'

'Sir? Please! No more sirs. Call me Patrick.' The Minister looked pained. He held up a hand. 'You and I, Joshua, belong to the same family now. We are, so to speak, blood brothers. So no more sirs!'

'Talking of which, how is my favourite sister?'

They spoke for the next few minutes about family matters before the Minister brought the meeting back to Captain Mbote's telephone call of the day before.

'I've done some checking,' he said. 'And as you know, your Corporal Tembo Mbali's wife and daughters died in a village massacre some weeks ago. They never found the son's body so we presume he's still alive. No one knows for sure who did it but it's rumoured that the God's Freedom Army faction were to blame.'

He put the tips of his fingers together and studied the Captain intently. 'So your story of the meeting you had in the Hotel Splendide interests me on many levels. Tell it to me again.'

When the Captain had finished, the Minister got to his feet and began pacing up and down. 'The key points in your story are surely these,' he said. 'The boy this man Morrell told you about is most likely to be Corporal Mbali's son. Sam is the boy's name. So that rings true. Then the name Colonel Dada crops up. And that fits in with what little we know about the massacre. It also interests me in a strategic sense.'

He went to the window and looked out. 'What is Dada doing so far out of his own tribal area, up on the

Baruba River? He's running a big risk tangling with the local warlords, especially if he stays there for much longer. He might have already moved on by now of course, but it's what he was doing there that intrigues me.' The Minister went back behind his desk. 'Now let me tell you why your call has been so important to me.'

He pressed a button on his desk and his aide appeared. 'Get me the file on Jean Morrell.' Then to Mbote, 'That is the man you met yesterday afternoon, right?'

Captain Mbote nodded.

'This is all we have on him,' the Minister told him some moments later. He pulled out a single sheet of paper. 'It's official confirmation of his UN role in this country and his job responsibilities.' The Minister tapped the sheet of paper. 'On here it appears that Morrell is a qualified mining engineer with two years' practical experience in Malawi. So he's no fool.'

'He told me his father had been a soldier,' Mbote put in. 'And said I wouldn't want to know any more about it.'

The Minister scowled. 'His father was an old white supremacist named Paul-Henri Morrell. He was a leading mercenary in the 1970s and part of a five-hundred strong so-called commando, led by an even

155

nastier man called Schratte. This man, Jack Schratte, is alive and still busy meddling in African affairs.'

'You think these things are all connected?'

The Minister nodded. 'Something's going on, I'm sure of it. Morrell has already flown to Brussels twice this year. Officially, he's been on leave. A week ago he returned, accompanied by a much older man. They immediately flew up-country in a chartered plane. We know nothing about where they went, who they met and why they came in the first place.'

'Majunga is a big place,' Captain Mbote told him. 'It is easy to disappear.'

'Especially when foreigners bribe our immigration officers to look the other way. Both coming and going!' the Minister added angrily.

'But what do we do about Sam? We can't just leave him—'

'Joshua,' the Minister interrupted. 'We think and hope he's alive. But that's all. We still don't know where Dada is. Do I have to remind you of the army's total failure so far to locate him?'

Captain Mbote shuffled his feet. 'So, what do we do?'

'Give me time. I'll work something out. However, let me now give you the government's official line.' He rapped the top of his desk with his knuckles.

'You will not tell Corporal Mbali anything at all. Not yet. I don't want rumours starting. If Dada was to hear, he'd kill the boy without a moment's hesitation. Your commanding officer will be told, but that is all. No one else must know until I say different.'

'But this man, Jean Morrell. He must know a lot more, surely?' Captain Mbote insisted. 'Can't we pressure him? Question him?'

The Minister nodded. 'At the right time, yes.' He paused to pick his words carefully. 'The trouble is, Joshua, that this whole matter is becoming very political. Some people in this government don't seem to mind who we do business with. And there are many more things at stake here than you have any right to know about. You're going to have to trust me. And remember, not a word about any of this to anyone. Too many people's lives may depend on that.'

CHAPTER 25

An aide peered around the door.

'Yes! What is it?' snapped the Minister.

'It's the President, sir,' the aide told him breathlessly. 'He'd like to see you when you have a moment.'

'That means now,' the Minister said and reached for his jacket.

The President's office was huge. Photographs of him shaking hands with world leaders stood on a grand piano at one end of the room. His massive desk was uncluttered except for a computer and a single telephone. The Minister stood in front of the desk and waited.

The President looked up. 'I understand you're investigating the curious case of the boy Sam, Colonel Dada and my old friend Jack Schratte?'

The Minister's jaw dropped. 'You know these people?' he managed to say.

The President shrugged. 'Some of them. The Belgian, Schratte, I know quite well. Who doesn't? He's a friend of ours. And useful.'

The Minister bowed his head and accepted the rebuke.

'The so-called "Colonel" Dada, I have never met. He's a monster and belongs to a tribe of well-known trouble makers. Enemies of ours. The sooner he's done away with the better. As for young Sam, he's just a simple village boy who, if he lives, will spend the rest of his life herding goats.'

'Like President Obama's grandfather,' the Minister reminded him.

The President smiled thinly. 'Possibly. But far more important for us, Sam is from the East of the country. One of us. So are most of the Majungan Rifles. We've elections coming up next year and you never know when you might need the army in a democracy like ours.'

The Minister nodded and looked thoughtful.

'Stay close to me, Patrick.' The President smiled. 'And you'll have a full belly every day of your life. I know you've been to business school in the States but there's a lot to be said for the way we do things back here.'

The President waved him to take an armchair. 'For instance, it's time we got rid of Dada. He's done what we needed.'

'Needed? I'm confused.'

'Then listen,' the President told him. 'Let's say Jean Morrell finds gold up on the Baruba River. He goes to see Schratte, whose experts confirm the find is the real thing. Good quality. Schratte contacts us. We agree a plan. Dada is offered a big piece of the action and can't resist it. He moves in and stakes his claim. Contacting Dada, by the way, was Morrell's job. Didn't he do well?'

The Minister could hide his impatience no longer. 'But where do we come in?'

The President laughed. 'Dada and Schratte officially share the profits fifty-fifty. In reality, Schratte will only take ten per cent of his cut. He gives us the rest. The government. But times are changing. There's an election soon. We need a lot more money. We have to build hospitals. Clinics. That sort of thing. So now we need to control those gold diggings one hundred per cent.'

'How?'

The President looked up at the ceiling. 'That brother-in-law of yours, Captain Mbote. Smart man. Could make General in the not too distant future.

Provided you keep your own place on the greasy pole, of course. Where was I? Oh, yes. The army.'

He shifted in his chair. 'Now we know where Dada is, we send in the army to destroy him. We then return the diggings to their rightful owner. The people. We tell the world press we're getting rid of a bloodthirsty warlord and freeing our captive children.' He laughed. 'It's a winner. A good story out of Africa! They might even put me up for a Nobel Peace Prize. Neat, eh?'

The Minister made a face. 'There'll be an awful lot of people killed,' he protested. 'Especially children. That'll cause us trouble abroad.'

The President shook his head. 'Not if we position it right. If this boy Sam has any smarts, we could use him as a spokesman for the children. If he's any good, the international press will lap him up.'

'But how do we find him? Sam, I mean. We don't even know if he's still alive.'

'I've thought of that,' the President reassured him. 'This is what you do. Call Morrell in and tell him he's got to get very close to the boy. He needs Sam to ride bodyguard or liaison. Something like that. When he's got him, he then hands him over to us.'

'And if Morrell refuses?'

'Then we file an official complaint about him to the

UN in New York. Accuse him of child trafficking. Something nasty.'

'So we get the boy back and reunite him with his father. And the army keeps busy and happy,' the Minister said.

'Now you're talking. You know how simple minded soldiers are. Getting Sam back will thrill them to bits. New excuses for more parades. Promotions all around.'

He looked at his watch and stood up.

'How old is that official car of yours?'

The Minister thought. 'The Mercedes? Two years. Three at the most. Why?'

The President chuckled and put an arm around his shoulders. 'Patrick! You're on to a winner. Get this sorted out and you'll see just what a good friend Mr Schratte can be. You wait and see!'

CHAPTER 26

Sam and Kito stood in line, waiting for breakfast. The cookhouse was just two walls and a sagging tin roof. An old army cooker had been dug into the ground and a jet of flame roared away under a row of battered metal containers. Sparks flew high into the grey half light of the new day. It was not long after dawn but there was no joy in the sky. Instead, dark clouds pressed down on the earth, squeezing all the energy out of the new morning. The air was oppressive. Sweat glistened on the boys' faces as they shuffled forward.

Every morning at eight o'clock Colonel Dada held a parade which everyone attended on pain of punishment. Depending on his mood it might last for an hour. At other times, especially if he was busy with his schemes or even hung-over, it might take only a few minutes. Sometimes he lectured them about his beliefs. Occasionally he told them what was happening in the outside world. Most of the child soldiers watched him with dead eyes, waiting for prayers and the final blessing.

Captain Simba, not to be outdone, insisted on his boys parading a quarter of an hour before this. He marched up and down, trying to instil in them a smarter military bearing. In fairness, his boys did look a cut above the others when on parade.

Kito put his hands in his pockets and yawned.

'Bet you never got up as early as this back in your village.'

'I did! Every day,' Sam told him indignantly. 'I lit the fire and took the animals out.'

Kito scratched an armpit. 'How many animals did you have?'

Sam smiled, remembering. 'A strong milk cow and sometimes a calf. We had the best cow in the village. And dozens of goats. How about you?'

'I never had anything to do with our animals,' Kito said. 'That was girls' work. My sisters looked after them.'

He stopped as Captain Simba appeared. He had been jogging. He did this every morning. He came running up calling out 'Good mornings' to everyone as he barged his way through the waiting boys. He rubbed Sam's head as he passed.

The line shuffled forward. Raindrops dripped from the roof of the cookhouse. Four more adults pushed past the boys. Sam stood back to let them pass. The men ignored him. They were members of Colonel Dada's personal bodyguard and considered themselves an elite force. They kept themselves entirely to themselves.

'Morning, Sam!' one of the cooks called. 'And how many eggs would you like today?' She laughed good-naturedly and dumped a ladle of mahindi* porridge on to his tin plate.

Sam grinned back. It was always porridge for breakfast, but he didn't mind. Just as long as it wasn't his turn to wash out the huge cook pots. That meant lugging them down to the river and at least an hour's work there, cleaning them with sand. There was a very real sense of danger down by the river. While a child soldier always went with him as a guard, Sam kept his own gun very close to hand. And his eyes wide open. One of the men soldiers had told him never to go to the same place two days running. 'Crocodiles watch

* Mahindi: the Swahili name for maize.

165

you,' he had told Sam. 'You go to the same place at the same time and one day soon, they waiting for you. Then it's too late.'

The river was at least a hundred metres wide and its surface was broken with rocks and sandbanks. Reeds fringed both banks. Perfect cover to hide in. Sam did not envy the women who went there to do the washing.

Kito nudged him. 'I was talking to you,' he complained. 'You been listening with half an ear again,' and he laughed.

They finished the porridge, licked their spoons and made their way back to the huts. 'Another happy day,' Kito grumbled, lying on his camp bed. 'Good times I have known. I heard Dinka say that we're doing another village any day now. How you feel about that?'

Sam ignored the question. He had heard the same rumour and it made him feel sick. He put a hand in his pocket and pulled out five small black pebbles. 'Like a game?' he asked.

They played jacks, gently throwing the stones up in the air and seeing how many they could catch on the backs of their hands. They were engrossed in this until it was time for the morning parade.

All heads turned to watch Colonel Dada appear.

One glance would tell them what sort of mood he was in. Captain Simba eased forward and wiggled his toes in anticipation. Colonel Dada was pure dynamite. You never knew what he would do next. And the Colonel did not disappoint him that morning!

Colonel Dada burst through the bead curtain with an AK-47 in his hand and shouted, 'God is my friend!' at the top of his voice. Then he fired off two full magazines. The first was at a line of crows perched along the roof of the hut opposite. The second magazine zipped high over the heads of the boys on parade. Some of the most recent arrivals ducked or threw themselves to the ground. Then, Captain Simba and other unit commanders ran around, kicking and slapping them upright again. When he had finished firing, Dada went back inside his hut and reappeared a couple of moments later, this time holding his cross.

He walked briskly towards the waiting parade, stopped ten metres away and blessed them.

'He's in a good mood,' someone muttered. 'Wonder what he's been smoking?'

'Stop talking!' Captain Simba hissed from the side of his mouth.

Colonel Dada surveyed them and shook his head as if in sorrow. 'I see too many unhappy faces all around me,' he began. 'Sad faces everywhere. They show me that your hearts are troubled. Is it because it is raining? Tell me.'

He put a hand to his ear in elaborate pantomime and pretended to listen. No one moved or said anything. All eyes were fixed on this terrifying man who had the power of instant death over them all.

'Lift your faces to the sky and prepare to give thanks that you have seen this day,' he shouted. He raised a hand. 'I have good news for you all. Good news that will help us fulfil our mission here.'

This time, a buzz of expectation ran through the ranks of the children and disappeared out into the surrounding wilderness. Colonel Dada threw both arms wide. 'We are going to become . . . RICH!' he shouted. '*Very* rich – and all of you will share in our success.'

Kito snorted. 'Must be bank-robbing time again.'

Colonel Dada looked around at them, his head swinging from side to side like a mamba. 'Friends of ours, *good* friends of ours,' he continued, 'have found gold very close to here.' He paused to let the words sink in. 'And we are all going to share in their good fortune.'

'Does that mean we can go home?' Sam asked, but no one seemed to hear him in the general hubbub.

Colonel Dada was shouting again. 'All of you will have new uniforms, new weapons.'

'A radio?' someone called out.

'And a personal radio,' agreed Dada, whose hearing was acute. 'Everyone will have a personal radio.'

'Sunglasses?' shouted another.

The Colonel smiled. 'And sunglasses. Whatever you like.' He held up a hand for silence. Captain Simba looked round fiercely to make sure his boys were paying proper attention.

'There will be changes in the way we do our work,' he went on.

Dinka snorted but said nothing out loud.

'From now on,' continued Colonel Dada, 'we will be guarding the diggings against all intruders and enemies. We will protect the miners personally, and make damn sure they hand in all the gold they find. That will be your job. The sin of theft will not be tolerated. Under pain of death!'

He beckoned to Captain Simba to step forward and put a hand on his shoulder. 'This man, our well-loved and trusted Captain Simba, will be in charge of discipline and security at the gold diggings.'

Captain Simba beamed with pleasure and Sam found himself cheering with all the rest of the boys. There was one more unexpected piece of news.

'It is time we had a party,' Colonel Dada told them. 'Tomorrow night we will celebrate. The cooks will give us special food. I want enough palm wine and beer for everyone. We must thank God for our good fortune.'

CHAPTER 27

Early the next morning, the cooks were hard at work preparing for Colonel Dada's party. As Sam and the others waited, Penda, the most friendly of the cooks, was pounding cassava with a heavy wooden paddle.

'Making flour,' she told them, 'to make the bread.'

'What else we having?' someone asked.

'We giving you oluwombo and chicken, bush meat and any fish we can get from the river,' she said. 'Frogs' legs too, if we can find where the frogs are hiding.'

'What's "oluwombo"?' another asked.

'It's goat meat, peanuts and plantains all cooked together,' she said.

'What about simbriki – bush rat?' Sam said.

'Cheeky boy! Nothing wrong with simbriki,' Penda told him, with a wink. 'Full of goodness. I give it to you boys all the time.'

Later that morning most of the men soldiers assembled outside Captain Simba's hut. They were going to tap the trees from which palm wine was collected. The men carried sturdy bamboo poles to use as ladders. Sam tagged along and volunteered to carry as many large plastic bottles as he could manage. When they reached an oil-palm tree, one of the men swarmed up the pole, cut a small hole in the trunk just below the fan of leaves, then tied a bottle to the trunk. The liquid soon came seeping out.

'You a palm wine drinker, Sam?' Captain Simba asked.

Sam wrinkled his nose. 'It's got a sour taste,' he objected.

'Ah!' said Simba. 'That's because you drank it too late. The longer it waits the sourer it gets. And the stronger!'

He shouted to one of the men high overhead. 'Sam's coming up. Let him taste some.'

The man waved in acknowledgment. Sam took the bamboo in his hands. He felt its smoothness and licked his lips. Climbing this wasn't going to be as easy as it looked.

He remembered the way the man had done it, gripped the pole firmly between his knees, then reached as high as he could and pulled himself up. It reminded him of a toy he had seen a child in his village playing with, months ago. After a couple of heaves, he forgot to worry about how high he'd have to climb. The effort was taking all his concentration.

When he reached the top, he waited while the man lifted the bottle and tilted it towards him. The liquid inside was frothy and looked like milk. Sam was surprised how much was already in there. Quite a lot of it splashed down his chin but he managed to drink a mouthful. To his surprise it was very sweet and tasted like coconut water.

'Too much will make you very drunk,' the man said, with a grin. 'And wash your face,' he shouted after Sam, 'or the bees will lick it off for you!'

'We'll come back later and collect it,' Simba said, when they eventually finished.

Everyone was good humoured as they made their way back. Some of the men began to sing. As they reached the compound, Captain Simba drew Sam to one side. 'Sam, go find Dinka for me. And come back too. I want to talk to both of you.'

Dinka was sitting on a low wall.

'Captain Simba wants to see us.'

Dinka cleared his throat loudly and spat. He got to his feet and took a last drag from the cigarette he was holding. Then he flicked it away. 'He likes you, doesn't he?' he stated.

Sam wasn't sure what the boy meant. Dinka was smiling at him but there was no friendship in his eyes. In silence, they walked across the compound to Simba's hut.

'Got news for you. Big news,' the Captain greeted them. 'You heard the Colonel making me his number one right-hand man yesterday?'

Sam nodded.

This time Captain Simba spoke directly to Dinka. 'It's going to mean changes for you as well as me.' He paused. 'Dinka, from tonight, you in charge of my unit. Captain Simba's Boys. My pride and my joy. So you treat 'em well.'

Dinka gave a little nod to show he had heard but said nothing.

Simba looked down at Sam. 'And you, Sam, I want you to become Dinka's number one boy. Understand?'

Sam's eyes widened. He could hardly believe it. Why him? What had he done to deserve it? And what would it mean? In a daze, he mumbled his thanks. For a moment he was tempted to ask what Dinka did for most of the time, then quickly decided he'd find out soon enough. In the meantime, the realisation that this was an honour he was being given sent a rush of pride coursing through him.

'Does that mean I'm a sergeant?'

Captain Simba considered. 'Sort of. Yes. Why not?' And he laughed.

'So I become a captain?' Dinka said matter of factly.

This time Captain Simba looked embarrassed. He shook his head. 'Only Colonel Dada can make you a captain. You know that.'

'So how about lieutenant?' Dinka demanded.

'I suppose so,' replied Simba, uncertainly.

'Will you tell the unit at tomorrow's parade, so everyone knows?' Dinka asked.

Captain Simba shrugged. He looked pointedly at the watches on his arm. 'Time for me to be seeing Colonel Dada for a proper briefing. You can dismiss now.'

Later, Sam asked Dinka, 'What do you want me to do?'

Dinka stared at him. 'You just do everything I say.' And he walked away.

CHAPTER 28

Night comes quickly near the equator. Twenty minutes after sunset, it is dark. Sam took out a box of matches and lit the hut's solitary paraffin lamp. He adjusted the wick and hung it on a nail in a beam that ran across the middle of the room. Shadows danced over the child soldiers' bedrolls and their few possessions. There were flickers of movement in the far corners as the rats left their holes and began their search for food. Sam saw their eyes gleaming and heard impatient squeaks. When he had first arrived, some of the children used to blaze away at them for fun with AK-47s. Then someone had been blinded by a ricocheting bullet and Colonel Dada had forbidden the practice.

Sam left the rats to get on with it and stepped outside into the warmth of the African night.

The moon was already up and high overhead. The compound throbbed with activity. A generator hummed noisily and Sam wondered where it had come from. As he walked, rows of light bulbs suddenly came on. It was the first electric light Sam had seen since his kidnapping. For a moment he was dumbfounded then he clapped his hands in excitement. He was not the only one. Everywhere there were cries of pleasure and loud clapping. Sam's eyes shone.

One line of bulbs reached Colonel Dada's hut. Others were looped through tree branches across the middle of the compound. A third cable took light out to the cookhouse. Sam could hear the cooks singing and laughing in high good humour. In sheer exuberance he began to run. He chased his shadow across the ground with his arms outstretched like an aircraft until a man shouted at him to help move Colonel Dada's ceremonial chair into the middle of the platform.

By the time that had been done, the compound had filled up with people. The illuminated area in front of the platform would later on be cleared for dancing. Right now though, the cooks were bringing down large cooking pots and heaving them on to the row of tables that stood waiting there. On the other side of the platform, Captain Simba and some other men were filling tin mugs with palm wine and beer. Everyone was talking loudly and there was even laughter. An unusual sense of well-being and comradeship hung over everything. Sam suddenly felt tearful and knew exactly why; it was just like being back home. A lump formed in his throat. He stepped back into the shadows and rubbed his eyes.

The next moment, gunfire crackled overhead in disciplined volleys. There was an audible gasp and everyone turned to stare as Colonel Dada came down the stairs of his hut, accompanied by his bodyguards. The Colonel was naked from the waist up and, even from where he stood, Sam saw that he had muscles like a bull. He had oiled his body so that the muscles flexed and stood out as he walked. His rifle was slung across his shoulders. Around his neck, he wore a large medal on a wide striped ribbon. It was shaped like a star. The bodyguards escorted him to his chair and took up their positions behind it.

Colonel Dada stood facing the crowd, bowing on all sides to the applause led by Captain Simba. After a while, he held up his hands for silence.

'Eat! Drink! Obey me! That is God's command to you all,' he called.

The bodyguards fired another volley into the night sky and the Colonel sat down. He accepted a plate of food from one of the cooks and immediately began to wolf it down.

Later that evening, Sam squatted on the ground next to Kito. The electric lights had gone out some time ago when the generator failed. There had been a sudden flash then darkness, while a cloud of foul-smelling smoke drifted across the compound. The bodyguards had unslung their rifles and peered around uncertainly, until paraffin lamps were produced and placed on the platform.

Most of the child soldiers had drifted away after that. A small number did stay, drinking beside one of the huts. Every now and then one of them would get up and bend over a table. Sam watched them, puzzled. 'What are they doing?' he asked.

'Brown-brown,' said Kito. 'Cocaine mixed with gunpowder. Supposed to make you feel very, very fierce.'

'You tried it?' Sam asked.

'Twice. The first time it made me sweat all over like I'd been in the river or something.'

'And the next time?'

Kito made a face. 'Stomach cramps. Man! I couldn't stand up straight for two days.'

Sam chuckled. 'Dinka's with them,' he confided.

'Been there all the time.'

'Bye bye Dinka then. You're lucky. You won't see him for a week.'

Colonel Dada and his bodyguard were now sitting together on the platform, talking amongst themselves. Captain Simba stood nearby. There were a couple of other adults still dancing. A man was playing bongo drums very softly and another was crooning an old song. Sam saw Penda waving at him and he waved back. Everyone else was sitting on the ground looking relaxed.

'Take a walk?' Sam suggested to Kito. 'Only I'm not tired and I don't fancy rats running over me when I'm wide awake like this.'

'Sure. Why not?' agreed Kito.

They crossed the compound, avoiding Dinka and his friends. They stopped at the cookhouse. Two large rats were feeding there. Sam unslung his AK-47. Kito put a hand on his arm. 'Don't. You'll panic the sentries.'

Sam gestured with his rifle and the rats scuttled away.

'You don't like those things do you?' Kito said. 'You're always going on about them.'

'No. I don't,' Sam agreed. 'My father says that more men die in the army from disease than from bullets.

And rats spread disease everywhere.'

They walked past the cookhouse and on a further fifty metres until they stood facing the open bush. It was like a chequer board, Sam thought. Trees and bushes and patches of high grass, brilliantly illuminated, with shadows like pools of black water stretching silently in between. Away from the shadows, the ground dazzled like the whitest river sand.

He was just going to say something, when Kito nudged him and put a finger to his lips. 'Listen,' he mouthed.

Sam put his head on one side and listened very carefully. Kito was right. It sounded like someone snoring, and not very far away. Silently, he followed Kito. Twenty metres further on they saw a figure stretched out on the ground.

Instinctively both boys raised their weapons and approached cautiously. Kito gave an exclamation. 'It's old Sekou! What's happened to him?' He knelt down beside the man and peered at him intently.

'I know Sekou,' agreed Sam. 'He's all right.'

'He's drunk,' Kito said, clearly alarmed. 'Dead drunk.'

'But he's on sentry. He can't be.'

'Well, he is. And he'll be a dead sentry if Dada hears about it!' Kito slapped the man's face. The snoring stopped for a moment then continued unchanged.

'What do we do now?' asked Sam. 'Someone's going to find him.'

Kito thought for a moment. 'We've got to sober him up, and fast.'

'Water!' cried Sam. 'Lots of it. Pour it over him.'

'The cookhouse,' Kito agreed. 'There's always some there. Come on!'

But as they got to their feet, they heard a sound that made them freeze. It was the unmistakable 'snick' of a weapon being cocked. Someone had just eased back the working parts of a rifle and loaded a bullet into the firing chamber. And that someone was out in the scrub in front of them.

CHAPTER 29

Kito and Sam stared at each other, eyes big with fear. Sure of what they had heard. Praying that despite this, they were somehow wrong. They were two crouching figures, afraid to move in case the moonlight betrayed them. Terrified to provoke whatever it was out there beyond the anthills. And as they waited, they heard the sound the planet makes as it spins through space and time. And their eyes grew bigger and their skin crawled.

What if it was the army? Sam thought. Riflemen from his father's own unit? Getting ready to attack and free them? What should he do? Should he shout out and tell them it was only Sam and his friend Kito?

They heard a child's voice curse and then complain

and the spell was broken. They knew for certain now what was going to happen. Kito grabbed Sam's arm. 'I'll go tell Simba. You wake your boys. Go!'

As Sam ducked down and scuttled back to the cookhouse, he remembered Captain Simba showing them how best to use cover. The man had been so right. Simba really did know what he was doing and Sam wouldn't let him down now. No one shouted after him. No bullets followed his frantic scramble. He reached his hut safely and stood gasping for breath on the threshold.

'Who's that?' a voice called from the darkness.

'It's Sam! Sam! Get up! We're being attacked. Wake up! Wake up!'

He rushed around the room, feeling for bodies, shaking them, kicking them awake. He was surprised how quickly they responded.

'What's happening? What's wrong?'

'Enemies! In the bush. Out past the cookhouse. Kito and me. We hear them. Get your guns and follow me. We've got to stop 'em!'

He ran outside, cocking his own weapon. He looked around the compound. There was no one to be seen and no sign of life anywhere. 'Come on!' he urged the others. 'Hurry!'

He reached the cookhouse with the rest close

behind. 'Spread out in a line,' he urged. There was so much more he should be telling them. He knew that. But he lacked both the words and experience. Where was Kito? What had happened to him?

'Come on!' he urged them and ran forward.

Beyond the cookhouse, everything looked the same. Nothing moved. There was not enough wind to even rustle the grass. An owl shrieked into the silence. Sam's stomach heaved. What if there was no one out there? What if they had imagined it? Well, it was too late to worry about that now.

He put the butt of his rifle to his shoulder and fired. Behind him, there was a chorus of yells and a stream of bullets flicked past his head. He flung himself down. No sense being shot by your own side, he thought. From somewhere in the darkness beyond, there was a whoosh of flame, a loud bang and something violent rushed overhead. A split second later it exploded on the far side of the compound. Sam yelled loudly. The enemy was real. And was firing at them with a rocket launcher. He rolled on to his side and reloaded.

Now the firing seemed to be coming from all directions. Twenty metres in front of him, Sam saw bushes starting to shake. Then there were figures running at him. Firing at him. The flashes from their guns for an instant as bright as lightning.

He closed an eye and took aim at the nearest one. Bullets thudded into the ground beside him. A small branch fell across his back. There was sand in his mouth and nostrils. He must find better cover; he was too exposed here. He fired a long burst and saw someone fall.

There was more firing over to his left. He thought he heard Captain Simba's voice, so Kito must have found him in time. He saw two small figures running at him. Child soldiers like himself. He shot one who went down with a yell. He turned to face the other and realised he'd run out of ammunition. He threw himself to one side, scrambled up and ran at the child who dropped his rifle and fled, screaming.

Sam yelled in triumph and saw old Sekou sitting upright, holding his head in his hands. Without thinking, Sam snatched up the child soldier's AK-47 and thrust it at him. He bent and shouted in the man's ear, 'Get up, Sekou! It's your only chance! Get up and fight!'

A red flare burst high above them. It belonged to the enemy. It was a signal of some sort. He watched it drift down, trailing a thin plume of white smoke. There was a loud chatter from a machine gun followed by ragged cheering. He watched Sekou stumble forward, gun in hand. And wondered what had happened to Kito.

He recognised some children standing nearby. They belonged to the other huts. The moon went in behind a cloud, leaving a shadow that raced ahead of him towards a hulking figure that blocked his path.

'Sam!' shouted Captain Simba. 'You done good! Again!'

As the dawn light strengthened, they walked back together towards the compound.

'Who were they?' Sam asked.

'Ubique's people. The great "General" Ubique's rabble.' Simba spat. 'Some General! But thanks to you and that Kito boy, we're OK.'

'And Sekou too,' Sam added quickly.

Captain Simba looked at him and frowned, but said nothing.

Back in the compound, Simba walked across to a tree, where several people were lying unconscious. Dinka was one of them. He lay curled up, dead to the world. Captain Simba prodded him in the ribs with the toe of his boot. There was a tin mug in Dinka's outstretched hand. Sam looked at it and saw it was covered with small brown ants. He stared more intently and realised that Dinka himself was covered with them.

They were in his hair and ears. They were running over his face and the corners of his mouth. He looked like a corpse.

Captain Simba kicked him.

'This man has let me down. He has let us all down. He does not deserve any of the trust I put in him.'

He kicked Dinka again. The boy's body absorbed the blow.

Simba laid a hand on Sam's shoulder.

'I want you to be my unit commander, Sam. Captain Simba's Boys need you. You'll be their new leader. This thing,' he jerked a thumb at Dinka, 'is no longer part of us. To me, he's bush meat. I'll go tell Colonel Dada right away.'

Sam stared after him in dismay. This was the very last thing he needed. It was a disaster! The only thing he wanted to do was to escape. To slip quietly away when no one was looking and get as far away as possible from these people. And now this! He'd be at Simba's beck and call more than ever. And Dada's too. He was now 'one of them'. A trusted subordinate. A loyal follower. It was bizarre. And so unfair.

And what about Dinka? Dinka would sober up in time. How would he react when he found Sam had taken his job? The boy would be out for revenge. A bullet in the back would be almost a certainty, sometime in the not too distant future. He heard his name being called and saw Kito. Gloomily, he went to meet him.

CHAPTER 30

The telephone on Mr Schratte's desk flashed.

'I've the President of Majunga for you,' Martine said. 'Are you in?'

'Sure,' Mr Schratte replied. 'Put him through.'

He switched on a new recording machine, looked briefly out of the window at the rain, then, 'Good morning, Mr President! Very good to hear from you. What can I do for you?'

'These armoured cars of yours, Jack. How soon could you get them here?'

Mr Schratte sat back in his chair and considered. 'I can get them to you by sea but I'll need to charter a heavy-lift ship to do that,' he said. 'That'll take a week. Then to get them loaded, shipped to Africa and put on the railway all the way up to Majunga, I'd say a good four weeks more. Perhaps another week on top of that. Depends on how reliable the railway is these days.'

'And we'll also need to train up the military drivers and gunners,' the President added.

'That'll be another two weeks at least.'

'You said, "by sea",' the President said slowly. 'Is there an alternative?'

Mr Schratte smiled. 'There is. But it's very expensive.'

'Tell me.'

'There are a couple of ex-Soviet countries I have dealings with that still have suitable transport aircraft. The Antonov Condor, for example. I've already checked on this. Each aircraft can take twelve vehicles at a time. But,' he warned, 'as I said, it'll be expensive.'

'About the same as a couple of months' takings from a promising new goldmine?' the President queried.

'I'd say three months' earnings to be on the safe side.'

The President thought for a while. 'And these aircraft could fly direct to our own airport?'

Mr Schratte nodded. 'Yes, sir. Best if they landed late at night. And if anyone asks, you could always say it was emergency aid. Restocking for the next natural disaster. That sort of thing.'

The President chuckled. 'I presume these fighting

vehicles will come with plenty of ammunition?'

'They will, sir. I can even throw in a couple of "advisers" if you like. Gunnery and driving instructors. I'd say four months' takings would cover everything. Do we have a deal?'

The President clicked his tongue. 'These vehicles – what are they? Russian?'

'No,' said Mr Schratte mildly. 'They're British. Scorpions. Ninety-millimetre gun. A few years old, of course, but hardly used. The country that originally bought them has gone quite the other way.'

'British is best,' said the President. 'Wasn't that what they used to say?'

Mr Schratte laughed. 'They did, and in this particular case they were right. They sold a lot of them to Nigeria and Tanzania—'

'OK,' the President interrupted. 'Let's go for it. Will you arrange everything as quickly as possible? Usual terms?'

'You'll have them by the end of next week,' Mr Schratte told him, raising his free hand in delight. 'Sounds as though things are moving at your end, sir,' he added.

'They are. Dada's already making far too much money. It is time to crush him.'

'Well,' said Mr Schratte, cautiously. 'Here's

something else for you to think about. Our new friends, the Chinese, are busy buying up half of Africa. So don't you think they might be interested in a joint goldmining venture with you?'

'You know them? You know who to see?'

'Not yet. But I will. Would you like me to arrange a meeting here, to sound them out?'

'No! Not yet. Let's wait until Dada is destroyed first.' He paused. 'That child, what's his name? The one I promised the army I'd get back.'

'Sam?' Mr Schratte prompted.

'Yes, that's the boy.'

'Morrell's agreed to get him away from Dada. So just tell him when you want it done, Mr President.'

They talked for a few moments more, then Mr Schratte replaced the phone. He stood in the doorway of Martine's office.

'Get your coat,' he said as she looked up. 'I'm taking you to lunch at the best restaurant in town.'

CHAPTER 31

During the morning, Sam heard news that made his heart sink. The excitement of the night had given way to a bad-tempered tiredness on everyone's part. There was rain in the air and the ground in the compound was turning sticky under foot.

'You've got to give evidence,' Kito told him.

'What's that mean?' Sam asked.

Kito shrugged. 'You've got to tell them how we found old Sekou.'

'You mean when he was . . .'

'Drunk.' Kito nodded. 'I have to as well.'

Sam's eyes widened. 'Who found out?'

Kito looked around. 'Simba did. Well, that's what they're saying. He found Sekou asleep under a tree not long after the attack ended. The children also saw him and they told Dada.'

'Stupid Sekou,' Sam groaned. 'He's the only adult here I like.'

'Me too.' Kito nodded.

'So what's going to happen?'

'To Sekou?' Kito looked at him almost in disbelief. 'They'll shoot him of course. Have to. I mean, if you and me had gone to sleep instead of taking a walk, we'd all be dead by now.'

Sam cursed and kicked the ground. 'What we got to do?'

'Colonel Dada's going to be the judge. It's up to him.'

'Where's Sekou now?'

'Tied up like a market chicken. But they'll be bringing him out soon. Listen!' There was a long burst of firing, then men's voices, shouting.

'Come on!' called Kito. 'Something's happening.'

They ran towards the platform and joined the others already crowding around it. There was no sign of Colonel Dada or Sekou. But Captain Simba stood up there, shouting at the crowd, gesturing at them to stand aside and make a pathway. Two cooks appeared, balancing a bowl of red-hot charcoal on long poles between them. The crowd shrank away.

'What's that for?' Sam gasped.

Kito shook his head.

One of the cooks now produced a long, thin knife. He made a slicing motion across his throat then put it down beside the bowl. There was another volley of shots and the children fell silent. Colonel Dada and his escort came down the steps of his hut and walked slowly towards the platform. Sam stared at his face and shivered. Even at this distance, Sam could sense the anger in the man. His eyes blazed and his body twisted to one side. He gestured at Captain Simba to begin.

'Fetch the prisoner,' Simba shouted. Sam stood on tiptoe to see better. The crowd gasped as Sekou appeared. There was a rope around his neck and his hands were forced up almost between his shoulder blades. There were guards on either side, their rifles pointing at his chest. Sekou's eyes bulged in terror and his tongue lay flat against the corner of his mouth. Sam had seen the same look in a terrified bullock, months earlier. Some of the crowd started jeering as he hobbled towards the platform.

Captain Simba shouted for silence, then turned smartly and saluted. Colonel Dada waved him away. He stared at Sekou and said nothing. Minutes passed. The crowd shifted from foot to foot then grew still. A breathless silence fell. Sekou started to sob. Great tears ran down his face and fell on his bare chest.

Colonel Dada walked to the edge of the platform and stood there looking at the crowd. No one said a word. No one sneezed or coughed or even fidgeted. The only sound was that of Sekou, crying.

Colonel Dada thrust out his arms and shouted, 'Sentries must act as everyone's eyes and ears. At all times. But especially when it is dark. Is that not so?'

He scanned the crowd intently as if searching for someone who might disagree.

'And anyone who fails in this duty to be our eyes and ears deserves to lose his own life. Do you agree?'

The crowd nodded and sighed in anticipation.

Colonel Dada folded his arms and stared at the ground. 'Now, because I am Colonel Dada the Merciful, I will give this sentry of ours a fair hearing.'

He bent towards Sekou.

'Sentry! Look at me!'

But Sekou began to shout incoherently. He lurched forward and laid his head on the floor of the platform, close to Colonel Dada's feet. One of the escorts raised his rifle. The guards dragged Sekou back and held him while he struggled.

Colonel Dada took a pace backwards. 'Sentry . . . I'm waiting!' he called. 'Did you fall asleep while on sentry duty? Because you were drunk? Answer me!'

In the terrible silence that followed, Sam listened to

197

Sekou's laboured breathing. The man tried to speak but the words stuck in the back of his throat.

'Sekou – are you guilty or not?'

The medals pinned to the front of Colonel Dada's soutane clinked impatiently.

'If you refuse to plead, then we must put you to the ordeal, and let God decide.'

He motioned to the cooks. One of them slid the knife into the middle of the glowing charcoal. There was a gasp and the crowd surged forward.

Colonel Dada stooped and picked up his cross. His voice became thoughtful.

'It may be,' he said slowly, 'that an evil spirit occupied your mind last night. Yes, that is possible.' He turned and pointed at Captain Simba. 'We go too fast. What evidence do you have of this man's crime? I need to know!'

Captain Simba took a deep breath.

'Colonel, sir. Two boys found him drunk. The same two boys who saved us from the attack. Sam and Kito.'

Colonel Dada considered this. Then he announced, 'Bring them here!'

Many hands grabbed at Sam and Kito and thrust them towards the platform. Awkwardly, Sam clambered up on to it. He was aware of Sekou standing tethered below him and looked away into Captain Simba's sweating face. He noticed how Simba's hands were shaking and realised he was frightened too.

'Well, get on with it!' shouted Colonel Dada. 'Get on with it!'

Captain Simba licked his lips. 'You boys! Where did you see Sekou?'

Sam and Kito looked at each other and hesitated. Then they both started to say something and stopped, uncertainly.

'Where did you see Sekou?' Captain Simba's voice rose.

'In the bush just past the cookhouse,' Kito told him.

'By a tree,' Sam added and felt a bead of sweat run down his side.

'What was he doing?'

'Looking out all around him,' Sam heard himself say and bit his tongue. It was a clumsy lie.

'He was awake, then?' Simba asked.

Sam hesitated. And trembled. What could he say next?

'The place where he was,' Kito put in quickly, 'was all in shadow. It wasn't that easy to see—'

He broke off as Colonel Dada strode towards them. 'If he was "all in shadow", as you say,' he cried, pointing

199

at Kito, 'then how did your friend here see him looking out?'

There was a horrible silence. Colonel Dada put his face close to Sam's and stared into his eyes. 'If you're lying to me, boy,' he said quietly, 'I'll have you beaten to within an inch of your wretched little life. Understand?'

Sam's body began to shake. He could no longer breathe. He thought he heard Kito cry out, 'No, sir! We only saw him for a moment. Honest!'

'Then you don't know if he was drunk or not,' Captain Simba added, bravely. He stepped close to Sam. 'They're both good boys, Colonel. Maybe they're a bit frightened by all this.' And he waved his hand at the crowd and then at Sekou.

There was another long silence. Sam felt Colonel Dada's eyes burning into his brain. Could the man read his thoughts? Could he see the hate that lay inside there?

Abruptly, Dada turned away. He jabbed a bony finger into Simba's chest. 'All for One and One for All, eh Captain?' He gave an unfriendly cackle. 'So was it you who found Sekou asleep and lying on the ground?'

Simba nodded slowly. 'Yes, Colonel.'

'And was he drunk?'

Captain Simba hung his head. 'Yes, Colonel.'

Dada strode to the edge of the platform and looked down at Sekou.

'If you plead guilty, you will be shot right away. But if you agree to the ordeal, you can still save yourself. I know everything about evil spirits. Maybe you were not drunk. Maybe the spirits cast a spell on you to make you appear drunk. Only the ordeal can prove your innocence.'

A large crow landed heavily on the roof of Colonel Dada's hut, with a loud beating of wings. It thrust its head forward and cawed three times. The Colonel pointed at it.

'Look! Baka!' he screamed. 'Look! The evil one has come back! The ordeal must begin. Open your mouth wide, Sekou. Put out your tongue.'

He jumped down on to the ground and held out his hand. The blade of the knife glowed red hot.

'Sekou,' he called. 'This is the knife of truth. I will pass it over your tongue. If you do not flinch, the evil spirit will leave you. Then you will no longer be possessed. You will be innocent and free to go.'

The crowd stared in fear – first at the crow, and then at Sekou.

Colonel Dada pushed Sekou's head back. 'Open your mouth!' And he held the knife just below the man's chin.

Sekou flung his head to one side and with a terrible howl jumped backwards. He turned, then lurched into the crowd and tried to batter his way through. The child soldiers, roused now to fever pitch, screamed at him and flung themselves on him. They tore at his face and eyes and clung to his legs. Sekou struggled on like a man wading through mud. His eyes were closed and his head was down. Like an old buffalo, he began to sway. His strength was fast running out. One last stagger and he sank under all their weight and lay face down on the ground.

'Guilty!' screamed Colonel Dada and, snatching up his rifle, fired at the crow. The bird fell off the other side of the roof in surprise and flew away, squawking loudly.

The Colonel's escort had meanwhile hauled Sekou to his feet and dragged him to the nearest hut. They thrust him against a wall and stood back, covering him with their rifles. As the crowd seethed around him, Colonel Dada reloaded his AK-47. He walked up to Sekou and shot him in the head.

'Throw him in the river,' he ordered. 'He does not deserve a proper burial.'

To Sam's horror he saw the Colonel looking at them and beckoning. Nervously, he and Kito approached.

'Come on! Come on! I am not going to eat you,' cried Colonel Dada, impatiently. Then he laughed and turned to his escort. 'Now there's a thought. We don't ever need to go hungry again. Greater love hath no boy!'

The escort laughed and slapped their sides. Colonel Dada put his hands on the boys' heads and blessed them in turn. 'Sam and Kito,' he said, 'I will remember you. Be good boys.'

CHAPTER 32

'Holy smoke! I don't believe it!' cried Jean Morrell, turning around in his seat to see more. 'This can't be the same place we stopped at before. Can it?'

His driver laughed. 'Sure is, Mr Morrell. Take a look at the GPS. Exactly the same coordinates as last time. We stopped right over there first time we ever came by. I made tea where that grocery store is now.' And he roared with laughter.

He was absolutely right, Morrell reflected. He peered through his window at the wooden shanty opposite. A woman was squatting down between large baskets of sweet potatoes and mangoes. There was an old tin box beside her where she kept her change.

The dusty, narrow road that ran alongside the Baruba River had been transformed. For most of the last kilometre, it was lined with bars and drinking dens, doss houses and shops selling everything from picks and shovels to fizzy drinks and cigarettes. Morrell had even seen a butcher's shop a hundred metres further back, with a telltale cloud of flies buzzing in front. And, everywhere, there were people. Hundreds of them. *More likely thousands*, Morrell thought. Most of them were men covered from head to foot in red mud. A great many of them carried a spade or a pick over one shoulder. Others balanced large plastic crates on their heads.

'I guess that's what they carry away the mud and rock in,' Morrell said.

The driver grinned. 'Don't tell me! I spent two years doing it. Then I got lucky and here I am now!'

Behind the line of rickety shacks, Morrell could see rows of battered trucks and the occasional parked four-by-four. Every day at dawn, these vehicles brought in miners from the outlying areas to the diggings. They returned home at sunset.

'Who'd have thought it?' said Morrell, shaking his head. 'Fancy taking a look at the diggings?'

The driver shook his head. 'I'll stay here, boss. Lot of thieves around.'

'I've never seen surface diggings before,' Morrell told him. 'I'm used to deep-level mining. Five hundred metres or more, below ground.'

The driver nodded. 'You're in for a shock, then. Very different here.'

They pulled off the road and bumped towards some other parked vehicles. Morrell got out and followed a crowd of miners headed for the diggings. He stopped on what was left of the high ground above the river and looked down in astonishment.

It was just like a First World War battlefield. Everywhere he looked, there were deep craters, most of them full of water. It was a huge, open pit. There was no sign of the river as such. It had been absorbed into the hundreds upon hundreds of diggings.

There were miners everywhere. Red ants that bobbed up and down. Some of them stood waist deep in water, digging feverishly and piling earth and mud into the brightly-coloured crates. Others formed human chains. They passed the crates along to another team whose job it was to dump the mud on to wide metal sieves and then rake through it. They were searching for gold dust, those small, glittering specks that might lie hidden somewhere in all this mud and loose earth. Still more men used clubs to smash open the larger pieces of stone. They were looking for a vein of gold.

Morrell had seen nothing like it in his life. He felt

like a drone, watching over this enormous hive of human activity. There was even the loud buzz of voices singing and calling to one another. He pulled out a pair of field glasses and studied the workers close up.

He saw people crouched beside small charcoal fires; their job was to mix the gold dust with nitric acid to separate any impurities. Only then could the gold be taken to Jack Schratte's or Colonel Dada's middlemen to be weighed and bought from the miners.

At this level, the miner's financial gains were extremely low. Striking gold for them was often a case of just bringing a single gram to the table. A gram might fetch anything from $7 to $20, depending on the international price. And that amount had to then be shared out amongst the whole team, once their own individual debts and charges had been paid for.*

Jean Morrell shook his head. It was not a way he'd want to earn his living. Not in a month of Sundays. He swept the glasses over the diggings and realised with surprise that the small, muddy figures he could see standing beside the miners, were child soldiers. Most of them had slung their rifles over their shoulders. Then he remembered that they were here to make sure

* Colonel Dada charged the miners $1 a day to work the diggings.

no one stole any of the gold.

Just below where he was standing, a man was tying a length of rope around his waist. Three others then began to lower him into a hole in the ground. It was a tight fit and only just wide enough to take the man's shoulders. Morrell now noticed that drier ground was pockmarked with similar shafts. He squatted down and stared intently.

'Two men die yesterday,' a man told him, noticing his interest. 'Tunnel collapse. They pull them out but it's too late. They dead.' He shrugged matter-of-factly. 'Happens,' he added and walked on past Morrell, down into the diggings.

Slowly, Morrell got to his feet. *Poor devils*, he thought. *What a way to live.* He couldn't even imagine himself doing it. Or what it must be like physically. Bending and digging for days on end in the hope of finding just a few grams of gold. And then having to face Colonel Dada's rapacious middlemen. And Jack Schratte's too, he remembered guiltily.

Feeling unusually sombre, he walked back to his Land Rover. It was time to visit Dada. And to do something about that boy, Sam. He cursed, gently. Sam was becoming a real pain. Jack Schratte, though, was insistent he got him away from the rebels. It was part of the deal he had made with the President of Majunga, for Pete's sake! It was easy for Schratte to bang the table, sitting back there in Belgium. But Dada was no fool. He was bound to wonder about Morrell's interest. What happened if he refused, point blank, to let the boy go? He had a sneaking feeling that Dada did not think much of him. Jean Morrell sighed. Perhaps Africa was not really the place to be. Well, not this part of it, anyway.

He reached the Land Rover and rapped on the driver's window. The man was asleep.

'Amazing place,' Morrell told him. 'Just like being on the moon.'

'Only wetter,' the driver agreed. 'Where now, boss?'

'The compound. Colonel Dada. He must be a happy man these days!'

The driver's teeth flashed. 'Very happy man.'

They drove up the long track that led to the compound. There were more lean-tos and shanties selling beer and food along here. A few women in brightly-coloured dresses came out to wave as they went past. As they reached the entrance to the compound, a heavily-armed man stepped forward and held up his hand.

Morrell showed him his UN pass. There was a delay while the man studied it. Then he waved them on.

'Glad to see they've increased their security,' Morrell

observed, as they drove past the line of bleached skulls on their wooden posts and two more sentries.

'It's all changed inside here,' the driver said, looking around. 'Where do we go?'

'Same place as last time,' Morrell told him. 'Dada's hut. Looks like he's stepped up his personal security too.'

The driver whistled.

'Brand new barbed wire,' he exclaimed. 'Wonder where he got that from?'

Colonel Dada's hut was almost unrecognisable. Double rolls of barbed wire surrounded the building. The windows had been barricaded over with planks of wood. The entrance was now hidden behind a head-high wall of sandbags. Another sentry, cradling a heavy machine gun, stood beside the narrow doorway.

Outside the wire, a queue of mud-covered miners waited. They looked in high spirits.

'Taking their gold dust in for weighing,' the driver said.

Surrounding them was a ring of child soldiers. Morrell thought they all looked very bored. He noticed a brand new Toyota land cruiser parked nearby. It was big and black and had tinted windows. It looked threatening. Morrell guessed what it was used for.

He remembered what Jack Schratte had told him a

few days ago. 'Remember that airstrip we used? Well, it's a wide open border. Couldn't be easier. Dada flies the gold into Uganda twice a week. All the big gold dealers live there. The dealers buy the gold from Dada, ship it up to Switzerland and sell it on the international market. They pay us. We say thank you. End of process. What could be more simple?'

Morrell wondered how much money was going into his own recently-opened account in Switzerland this month. That made up for a lot of things!

As he got out of the Land Rover, a child soldier ran up to him and thrust his rifle into Morrell's stomach.

'Hey! Stop that!' Morrell cried, shocked by the blow.

The boy shouted something at him and waved the gun in his face. It was obvious he was telling Morrell to put his hands up. Reluctantly, he did so.

'Let me through! I've come to see Colonel Dada. Colonel Dada. Colonel Dada! Understand?'

But the boy didn't. He stood his ground and shouted back.

'What's he saying?' Morrell demanded.

The driver shook his head. 'He's talking village talk.'

Morrell swore at the boy. He deliberately brought his hands down and made to walk past him. The boy yanked back the cocking handle and pointed a loaded rifle at him. He meant business.

'Stay cool, boss,' the driver warned.

Morrell smiled mirthlessly and watched as another boy, a boy he recognised with only half an ear, appeared from nowhere. There was a brief argument, then Sam seized the other's gun.

'Watch it! It's loaded,' cried Morrell.

Sam nodded. He took off the magazine and fired a shot into the sky. He then handed the rifle back to the boy.

'Hello, Sam,' said Morrell, holding out his hand. 'How have you been? You're just the chap I've been hoping to meet.'

He heard his name being called and turned to see Colonel Dada watching him from beside the sand-bagged entrance. Morrell was amused to see that instead of a cross, he now carried what looked like the very latest in satellite telephones.

'A very impressive operation, Colonel,' Morrell said, walking towards him. 'May I congratulate you?'

Colonel Dada looked up briefly then studied his phone.

'I've a present with me from Mr Schratte,' Morrell told him. He thought Dada nodded but couldn't be sure. The man had turned away. 'But I'd like to have a closer look at the diggings first,' Morrell called, raising his voice. 'Perhaps I could have an escort?'

He waited a little longer then asked, 'Can I take Sam here with me? I won't be long. I'll look after him.' And he tried to laugh.

Colonel Dada shook his head. 'Sam's in charge of security—' he started to say, when his telephone rang. He quickly checked to see who was calling and gave a little cry of delight.

'Colonel?' Morrell prompted.

'Oh, just take him!' Dada snapped, then began to listen enthusiastically.

CHAPTER 33

Captain Mbote listened to the briefing with rising excitement. This is what he had joined the army for. At long last they had the chance to lift the curse of Colonel Dada from the land. This was not going to be yet another training exercise with everyone back home in time for tea. No! This was for real and the whole regiment was involved.

He stole a quick glance through the open window. Out on the barrack square, he could see the thirty troop-carrying lorries drawn up in neat rows. Soldiers were hooking five-hundred-gallon water trailers to the backs of some of them. Three others were loaded with spare ammunition and mortar rounds. But pride of place went to the four recently-arrived armoured cars. He would be travelling in one of them himself and leading the assault.

He saw his own Sergeant Major looking busy and then spotted the recently promoted Sergeant Tembo, walking purposefully across the square. He looked good with those three stripes on his arm, Captain Mbote thought. But seeing him also reminded Mbote that there was still no news of the man's son. He had telephoned his brother-in-law, the Minister, last night for the latest news. According to Patrick, Sam was still with Dada in the rebel's camp.

'Let's hope no one has blundered,' had been the Minister's pessimistic take on the matter.

Captain Mbote thanked his lucky stars that he had still not told Tembo anything about rescuing Sam. There had been no point raising his hopes over something so uncertain. He turned his attention back to the briefing room. The Commanding Officer was summing up.

'So, to recap,' he was saying, 'the enemy are operating out of the old malaria hospital, one kilometre north of the current gold diggings.' He tapped a map pinned to a blackboard with his cane. 'Here, and here.'

He continued, 'A and B companies will surround the main compound by eleven hundred hours tomorrow morning. Make sure you stay out of sight of the compound itself. Then, on my word of command, you will advance on foot towards it.'

He looked over at Captain Mbote. 'Joshua, C company will advance up the track from the diggings. You will seize the compound and, in particular, capture Dada's headquarters.

'Go easy when you get there. And whatever you do, grab these so-called middlemen and guard them well. We'd also like Dada taken alive but if you have to shoot him, too bad.'

Someone asked a question. 'What about Dada's escort?'

The Commanding Officer smiled thinly. 'You can shoot them out of hand.'

Another officer stood up. 'Why don't we attack at dawn, sir? When most of them will be asleep?'

The Commanding Officer nodded. 'Good question.' He looked around at them. 'The President himself has requested that we keep child soldier casualties to an absolute minimum. I understand that by mid-morning, most of them will be out at the diggings, keeping an eye on the miners. So there'll only be Dada and his bodyguards left there. We'll arrest all those child soldiers who come back to the compound. We're taking rolls of barbed wire with us to construct a prisoner-of-war cage. That's where we'll put them to begin with. Any more questions?'

There were none. 'It's a three-hour drive to the compound. We leave at dawn tomorrow morning. Good luck, everybody!'

CHAPTER 34

'Hop in, Sam,' Morrell called cheerfully as they reached the Land Rover. Then to the driver, 'Let's get out of here, fast. Then find a quiet place off road. All right?'

The driver revved the engine and they moved off.

'So then, Sam.' Morrell turned around in his seat and looked at the boy. 'How's life with you?'

Sam thought a little, feeling flattered at the man's interest. 'We had an attack,' he said. 'At night. That General Ubique, I think. But we beat them,' he added, proudly.

'How long ago was that?'

Sam considered. 'Last week. At full moon.'

Morrell smiled at him. 'So you could see them, could you? That must have made things much easier.'

Sam frowned but did not reply. This man didn't

seem to know much about fighting in the bush at night-time. Probably, at *any* time. He sat upright on the back seat and held his AK-47 across his body. Still, Sam thought, he seemed a kind man, and kindness was a rare thing these days.

He looked out of the window, feeling a little embarrassed by Morrell's constant smile.

There were some buttons on the door beside him. Curiously, Sam pushed one. The window beside him opened with a loud whirring noise. Astonished and then worried, Sam looked at Morrell's face. The man was still smiling. Gingerly, Sam pressed another of the buttons. This time, the other rear window slid down. Sam laughed. He couldn't help it.

'You been in many cars, Sam?' Morrell asked.

'I been in one. Two times before. But not new like this.'

'Was that back in your village?'

Sam looked away. And said nothing.

'Back in Tshombe? Was that where the old car was?'

There was a long silence. Outside, the road was jammed with miners streaming towards the diggings. A motorbike scraped past, the driver handing himself along the side of the Land Rover. Morrell's driver banged the horn and made a rude gesture.

'We're losing our air conditioning,' he grumbled.

Morrell leaned over the front seat and brought both windows up again. Sam moved away from him, disturbed by the reference to his village. He realised, with something of a shock, that he had not thought about it very much for some time now. And that was awful.

'You been there?' he mumbled.

Morrell shook his head. 'No. I've never been. But I know somebody who has. Someone who knows you.'

Sam's body stiffened. What was this strange man trying to tell him? Was it some sort of trap? Tiny beads of sweat gathered on his face. He brushed them away and stared at Morrell. He swallowed hard and made a sudden grab for the door handle. Nothing happened.

'Sorry! We've got child locks still fitted, I'm afraid,' Morrell called. 'You can't open them from there.'

Sam flung himself back in his seat and stared at Morrell.

The driver coughed politely. 'This do here?'

They pulled off the road and stopped beside a very old baobab tree. Its branches hung straight down towards the ground like the bodies of so many dead pythons. Inside the ring of branches, it was very dark.

'You work for Colonel Dada?' Sam asked suddenly.

Morrell shook his head. 'No, I work for the United

Nations. In New York, America,' he added untruthfully.

'You are Colonel Dada's friend?'

Good question, thought Morrell. *Now what do I say to that?*

He stared at the boy, wondering how to proceed. Unless the rebels had totally brainwashed him, there was every reason to believe that Sam must hate Dada and everyone associated with him. But, and it was a big but, he had also read that a great many boys in Sam's position quickly transferred their trust to their captors. It was a matter of survival, Morrell supposed. Other experts, mainly doctors and experienced missionaries, thought there were darker forces at work. Perhaps it would be best to be upfront and honest.

'Sam! I've got wonderful news for you. Do you want to hear?'

The boy looked at him with expressionless eyes and said nothing.

Morrell took a deep breath. There was no place to hide now. This was it.

'Sam. Your father has asked me to bring you back to him. I can take you to him right now if you like.'

Morrell saw disbelief then happiness transform the boy's face. For a moment, his eyes shone. Then Morrell saw that light slowly fade. The boy's face crumpled and his shoulders sagged and the vehicle was full of the sound of unhappiness. Morrell let the boy cry until the driver became impatient and said, sharply, 'You stop making that row, boy. This gentleman's trying to help you. Don't you want that?'

Morrell reached around the front seat to put a hand on Sam's shoulder, but the boy knocked it away.

Morrell spoke urgently. 'The army's coming here, Sam. Your father's regiment. They're coming to rescue a lot of boys like you. Please believe me and come with me now.'

'I can't come *now*!' Sam shouted. 'I can't leave Kito. When Dinka hears, he'll kill him. I know he will.' And he began to rock backwards and forwards.

Morrell brought out a large red handkerchief and mopped his own face and neck.

'Who's Kito?' he demanded. 'Is he a friend?'

Sam nodded. 'He's my friend. He's my brother.'

Morrell felt a stab of pity for the boy. He thought quickly.

'Here's what we do,' he said. 'Sam. Listen! Tomorrow, find Kito. Keep him with you. We'll pick you both up in the morning. Early. Understand? Just tell me where to meet you and when. Can you do that?'

Sam sniffed loudly and stared at Morrell.

'You swear to me that this is all true? That my dad

really is coming here—?'

'It's true, boy,' the driver interrupted. 'It's all happening like Mr Morrell says it is.'

Sam took a very deep breath. 'Tomorrow, Colonel Dada takes the gold to the airplane. He always goes at the same time in the big, black car. Soon after breakfast.' He leaned over and pointed at Morrell's watch.

'About nine o'clock,' Morrell told the driver. 'Good! Now, where do we meet you?'

'On the track coming up the hill. By the beer store,' Sam told him, the words coming in a rush. 'I go there sometimes and get beer. The woman there is my friend.'

'I know it,' said the driver, nodding. 'It's got a big elephant sign outside. Yes?'

Sam almost grinned. 'It's called the Tembo Bar,' he told them.

'Well, let's hope it's a good omen,' Morrell said soberly. 'Now, we'd better get you back. Oh! And Sam . . . You must tell no one about tomorrow. No one. You understand? Not even Kito. Tell him tomorrow. But not before. Colonel Dada is very clever. So be careful!'

CHAPTER 35

Sam did not find Kito until late afternoon. He searched the compound from end to end and finally waited by the main entrance. He stayed there for the next hour talking to the sentries and looking down the track towards the diggings. A small, mud-covered figure eventually appeared and walked dejectedly towards them. It was Kito. Sam ran to meet him.

'What's happened? Why you so late? I have big big big news!' Sam told him, bursting with excitement.

Kito slouched beside him. 'I can't take much more of this,' he said in a low voice. 'I almost died today. It was only because Simba came along and took pity on me that I'm here now.'

Sam stopped and stared at him. 'Almost died?' He was shocked. 'And what's this "took pity on me" stuff all about? Come on! Tell me, cos I've got fantastic news.'

Kito waved him away. 'Sam!' he cried irritably. 'Leave me alone. Butt out, will you!'

They walked a further thirty metres in silence, then Kito mumbled, 'Only thing I want to do is get cleaned up. See you at the cookhouse.'

When they had finished their plates of groundnut stew, they walked a little way into the bush and sat down on a patch of sand.

'Now!' cried Sam. 'Listen to what's happened.'

'No! Wait!' Kito was clearly very angry about something. 'I almost died! Remember? So you listen to me for a change.'

'OK. Sorry.' Sam shut up and listened.

'I told you,' Kito explained. 'I've got this really nasty bunch of miners to watch. Well, this morning a new man joined. He came from somewhere up-country. Anyway, no one could understand much of what he said. He hadn't been a miner before and he was really slow. So they sent him down a new shaft they were digging.'

Sam smiled encouragingly and wished Kito would just get on with it.

'Do you know what they did to him? Guess.'

Sam threw up his arms. 'Tell me.'

'Well,' Kito continued, 'one of them, their boss man, the one with no teeth, caught a cobra. The next thing, he throws it down the hole on top of the man. And they all fall about laughing.' He shook his head in disgust.

'Was the man in the hole all right?' asked Sam, intrigued despite himself.

Kito swore. 'You stupid or something? What do you think? It bit him, of course. All over. He was screaming. He died soon after they pulled him back up. Blood and froth and stuff coming out of his mouth.'

Sam shook his head in disgust. 'Where was the snake?'

'At the bottom of the hole.'

'So what happened to you?' Sam demanded.

Kito picked up a pebble and threw it viciously at a lizard. 'Guess who came by and thought it a great joke?'

Sam shrugged. 'Who?'

'Dinka. He laughed so much I thought he'd wet himself.'

'Go on.'

'So then he sees me and gets nasty. Points his gun at me and tells them I'm a snake too.' He cleared his throat. 'Then he tells the men to put a rope around me. There's four of them. What can I do? One of them had a flashlight and they lowered it beside me. Then they let me down until I was about a metre off the bottom—'

Sam interrupted. 'And the snake? What was it doing?'

'It was squirming around, looking for a way out.' Kito put his face in his hands and shuddered. 'The worst thing was,' he went on slowly, 'every now and then, it reared up to check on the light. Then its head was level with my ankles.

'You know how I hate those things!' he suddenly shouted. 'All I wanted to do was to kick it. But if I had, I'd be dead too.'

'Oh, God!' wailed Sam.

Kito rubbed his eyes.

'How long did it go on for?'

Kito shook his head. 'For ever. Ten minutes. Half an hour? I don't know. Anyway, the next thing is I hear shouting above me. Then I'm pulled up and there's Simba looking really angry.'

'Not with you!'

'No. Not with me,' Kito said. 'He sacked the miners on the spot and kicked Dinka's backside all over the place.'

'He should have shot him,' Sam said.

'*I* will,' Kito told him. 'One of these days. Just wait.'

'If he doesn't get you first.'

'Or you, Sam,' Kito said soberly. 'You especially. You got his job. Remember?'

Sam nodded and suddenly felt exhausted by it all. Dinka, Simba and Colonel Dada. The whole damn lot of them. Well, they'd soon be people from the past. The nightmare was ending.

'Come on then!' Kito was saying. 'I'm flaked. I want to sleep. Tell me, what's your big news?'

Sam looked over his shoulder. 'We might be sleeping somewhere else tomorrow,' he said very quietly.

Frowning, Kito turned and looked at him. 'Sleeping where? Why are you whispering? I can hardly hear you.'

'I had a ride in that UN man's car today,' Sam told him.

'What UN man?'

'In the white Land Rover.'

Kito scoffed. 'Lucky old you. Know what I was doing? Only being bitten by snakes.'

'Listen!' Sam urged. 'He's on our side! He wanted to take me to my dad. Only I said you had to come too.'

Kito stared at him. 'Take you to your dad? Where? Why? Who is this man?'

'And his driver knows all about it, as well.'

'All about what?' Kito challenged.

Sam became impatient. 'Kito! The army's coming tomorrow. They're going to set us free.'

Kito shook his head. 'In that case, why does this man want to pick you up specially? It's a trap.'

Sam was getting angry. 'It's not a trap. I believed him.'

Kito got to his feet. 'Perhaps you wanted to,' he said, making a face. 'Look, it's getting dark. Time we went in.'

'Don't you believe me?' Sam shouted.

Kito stared at him. 'Tell me again. What's supposed to be happening? What did this man say, exactly?'

'We go to the beer store at nine o'clock tomorrow morning and wait for him to come.'

Kito laughed. 'And we can wave Colonel Dada goodbye on his way out to the airstrip.' He shook his head. 'Sam! I'm glad the man was nice to you. But I think you've imagined the rest of it.'

Sam nearly hit him. 'No! No! You got it all wrong.'

Kito yawned. 'Tell you the truth, Sam, I'll believe it when I see it. Tell me in the morning and I'll try and get my head around it. Good night!'

And he walked slowly back into the compound.

CHAPTER 36

Sam could not sleep that night. No matter how hard he tried, it was impossible. There was only one thing that mattered now and that was escape. Escape from Colonel Dada and his terrible people. Escape from this horrible compound where everyone lived on top of each other. And spied on each other. So he listened, wide awake into the small hours, to the cries and the nightmares of the sleeping boys, until they faded into a deeper unconsciousness.

He heard the rats grow bolder as the night wore on and followed the sound of their claws, tip-tapping over the concrete floor between the sleeping boys. And all the time, his mind soared and plunged in excitement and worry about the coming morning. And the longed-for prospect of seeing his father again.

Just before dawn, he went to the door of the hut and looked out. A cold mist trailed through the tree tops. Puddles of red mud were already forming. The steam rising from the cookhouse was the only sign of life. He listened to the thorn birds singing as they always did at this time of day. As they would tomorrow and the day after that. But he wouldn't be here tomorrow. He would never be here again. This was his last day!

His head began to spin and for a moment he had to cling to the door jamb. Then the sensation passed. He peered over his shoulder to see if Kito was awake. He could make out his body lying there, covered with a thin blanket. Should he wake him? What if he refused to come and meet the UN man? Or had told somebody else? But he quickly thrust that thought far from him. He wondered what would become of Kito in the future, after they had escaped.

He splashed his way towards the cookhouse to cadge a cup of bush tea. His friend Penda was the only person there.

'You heard the news?' she asked, handing him a mug.

'What news?'

'President Obama is coming to Africa.' She broke off to sing a few bars of a song, then, 'He's the first black President America has ever had. And now he's coming home to Kenya. How about that, my big soldier boy?' And she laughed and did a little dance.

Sam nodded, happy it pleased her so much.

'There's a future now for all us black people,' she told him. 'Sure, most will go on living like this. With all these wicked men telling us what to do. But wait and see, Sam, it's going to get better. One day it will even be better for folks like us.'

She started singing again. 'Know something?' she called. 'Today is the happiest day of my life.'

'Good!' Sam exclaimed. 'You deserve it.'

And she chucked him under the chin and smiled.

Colonel Dada was less sympathetic when they met an hour later. Sam was doing his best to keep out of his way but, as luck would have it, he walked straight into him.

The rain had stopped but it was still a miserable start to the day. Sam, unable as always to hide his feelings, grinned broadly.

'Wait!' Colonel Dada commanded and came closer to Sam. He stared at the boy, a puzzled expression on his face. He bent and peered into Sam's eyes.

'Happiness like yours is very unusual in a place like this,' he told him. 'Why are you so happy today, Sam, eh? Tell me, Sam. The truth now. There are no secrets between us, I trust?'

Ice-cold hands gripped Sam's insides. His mouth went dry and, worst of all, he couldn't think of anything to say. He stared at the man idiotically and wished he was a million miles away.

'Not in love, are we Sam?' Colonel Dada smiled. 'Love! Do you know what love is?' He cracked his knuckles. 'Sinful thoughts. You'll burn, Sam. Mark my words. There's a special place in hell for sinners like you.'

He made to walk away but turned quickly instead to face the boy again.

'And how was your little trip with our distinguished friend, Mr Morrell, yesterday?'

Sam stared at him, open mouthed. Did this man know everything? Had he already guessed? Sam was terrified.

'You didn't go to the diggings, did you, boy? Nowhere near them.' Colonel Dada's tongue flickered across his bottom lip. 'Where did you go, Sam? Only Dinka tells me that he saw Mr Morrell drop you back here but there was no fresh mud on your trousers. They were quite dry.'

His eyes skewered the boy. Sam was mesmerised. The man was like a black mamba.

'Is there anything you want to tell me, Sam?

Something only I might understand? I know all about evil. And treachery too. But in your case, I've not yet made up my mind.'

He reached out and seized Sam's remaining earlobe in his fingers. He pinched it, hard.

'You seem to be a good fellow. You're brave. But . . . there's something different about you today. There's a change I don't like. Come and see me the moment I get back. And bare your soul to me. I'll prepare a little test for you.'

Sam began to shake. 'Yes, sir,' he said weakly.

Later, he watched Colonel Dada and his escort drive out of the compound in the large, black Toyota. And was sick with relief by the corner of a hut.

'You better now?' Kito asked, coming to stand beside him. 'I knew it was something you ate.'

Sam wiped his mouth on the back of his hand and looked at him, blankly.

Kito dropped his voice. 'That stuff about the army and your dad.'

'You don't have to come if you don't want to,' Sam told him.

'You mean you're still going to the beer bar?' Kito looked at him almost in despair. 'What happens if he doesn't turn up?'

'He will,' said Sam. 'I just know he will. Coming?'

Reluctantly, Kito followed.

'The only problem now is Simba,' Sam warned. 'Watch out for him.'

'What about the sentries on the gate?'

'Leave them to me and don't say anything.'

They walked towards the main entrance. One of the sentries raised a hand in greeting. 'What you doing, Sam?' he called.

'Going to get beer for Captain Simba,' Sam told him. 'You want some too? Ain't no trouble.'

Another sentry appeared and grinned at him. 'What would your mammy say?' he called in mock horror. 'Hanging round beer bars at this time of the morning!' Both men laughed.

And then the boys were past and striding down the track.

'The sentries will see us hanging around, waiting,' murmured Kito. 'They'll get suspicious and come and see.' There was panic in his voice. 'Sam, for God's sake, what are we doing?'

Sam shook his head stubbornly.

'He said he'd be here and I trust him. Just do what I do.'

As they approached the bar, Sam waved at the owner. She was a very large woman in a saggy dress.

She looked at him and smiled.

'You an early bird, Sam. You want beer?'

'Later,' Sam replied, smiling at her. 'Only, we're waiting to meet somebody. Is there anything we can do to help?'

She nodded and looked pleased.

'You can move all the empty crates, if you like,' she said. 'From out the back to here in the road. Stack 'em five high. Got new stock coming today.'

They set to, working hard to distract themselves. Rows of empty crates began to build up on either side of the entrance.

'What's the time?' hissed Kito, glaring at Sam. He looked up guiltily as the woman came back in. She brought with her the smell of chicken frying.

'It's half-past nine,' she told him. 'When your friends coming? Only I got Colonel Dada himself eating here, at twelve. And I want everything tidy and out of the way for him.'

Kito dropped a wooden crate on his foot and yelled. Sam heard the sound of an engine approaching and ran to the open door. It was him! Mr Morrell in his distinctive white Land Rover. Kito crowded beside him in the doorway and watched, open mouthed, as the Land Rover pulled up in front of them.

'Sorry we're late,' Mr Morrell called, leaning over

236

and opening a rear door for them. 'But we had a puncture.'

'Those wheel nuts were rusted in real bad,' the driver complained, as the boys scrambled into the back of the vehicle.

'Where's the best place to turn around?' Morrell asked. 'Here or at the top?'

'Here!' Sam cried, beside himself with impatience. 'Quick! Please!'

The driver seemed to understand. He nodded and dragged the steering wheel hard over.

The woman came out to stare. She stood with her hands on her hips and looked puzzled.

'What about my crates?' she called, stepping on to the track. 'There're lots more!'

When she realised they were not going to stop, she became cross, and shouted after them, 'You wait till I see Colonel Dada. I'll tell him all about you boys. Running out on me like this!' She shook her fists and banged on the rear door of the Land Rover. Sam looked past her and up the hill. He thought one of the sentries was looking at them through binoculars.

'Right!' said Morrell. 'Let's get out of here, shall we?'

The driver gave him a look and took off with a jerk. Sam grinned at Kito and sank back into the comfort of the seat. He closed his eyes. They had done it!

'You two OK in the back there?' Mr Morrell asked. Then stopped, distracted by what the driver was saying. The driver was pointing a stubby finger at something ahead of them. Sam sat up and stared through the windscreen.

'Oh, God!' exclaimed Mr Morrell, as the large, black Toyota turned at the bottom of the hill and came barrelling up towards them. 'Oh, my God!'

CHAPTER 37

'Get down in the back!' the driver shouted. 'Get down. Behind the seats!'

Sam and Kito needed no urging. They burrowed down, their faces hard against the floor.

'You just stay there and shut up!' the driver ordered. 'Mr Morrell, sir. You make polite conversation with Colonel Dada. Look! He's stopping to talk to you!'

'Oh, God!' Morrell said again. But he was all smiles when the two vehicles stopped beside each other.

'Colonel! Good morning!' he called. 'And how are you today?'

Colonel Dada, not to be outdone in courtesy, bowed his head. 'Very well, thank you. But what brings you back here to see us again so soon?'

'I was looking for young Sam,' Morrell confided.

'We didn't see as much of the diggings yesterday as I would have liked.'

The driver was watching his wing mirror. A child soldier was running down the hill towards them. He was bigger than most. Quite a lot bigger.

'I'm so glad Sam seems to have found a patron,' Colonel Dada was saying, 'but I'm sorry to see he's not with you.'

The child soldier was not far from the Land Rover now. The driver put his hand on the gear stick. He had an instinctive sense of danger.

'No!' said Jean Morrell. 'He must be down at the diggings.'

'No! No!' echoed Colonel Dada. 'I'm sure he's not there. I wonder where he can be?'

'He's here!' Dinka shouted. 'He's in the back. Colonel Dada! He's hiding with Kito!' And he fumbled with his rifle.

The driver slipped the clutch and the Land Rover took off in a spray of mud. Behind them, Dinka's AK-47 rattled shots after them. One hit the rear bumper and ricocheted away with a shriek.

'God almighty!' shouted Mr Morrell. 'That was close. Well done, Driver. Brilliant! You saved us.'

'Not sure how long for,' the driver shouted. 'They're coming after us!'

'You boys keep down,' Morrell ordered.

'We got guns, sir. And we can fire real good,' Sam told him. He sat back up and looked behind.

The black Toyota looked like an angry bull. It had its lights full on and even Sam could see it was gaining on them. People were leaping out of the way as it thundered in pursuit.

'Faster!' shouted Mr Morrell as the driver took his hand off the horn to change gear. 'Faster!'

There were people, hundreds of them, watching with startled eyes. Not taking in what was happening. The driver braked fiercely. Sam and Kito pitched forward as the man swung the wheel to avoid two snarling dogs.

'Get on with it!' Morrell was shouting.

The driver gritted his teeth but said nothing. There was a loud bang and the rear window shattered. Pieces of glass flew everywhere.

'But we're the United Nations!' screamed Mr Morrell. 'They can't do this! I've got diplomatic cover.'

'You boys!' the driver shouted. 'Put your guns out the window and fire into the air to warn the folks ahead to keep out the way.'

Sam smashed his window with the butt of his rifle and poked the barrel through. He fired a long burst into the air. He could hear Kito firing on the other side. He snatched a look back. The Toyota was roaring after them. He fired at the shattered glass in the rear window and then at the vehicle behind. He thought he saw the Toyota lurch but it could have been a pothole.

'Keep that up!' shouted the driver. 'Give them something to think about.'

They were on the road that ran alongside the river. Colonel Dada's vehicle was about three hundred metres behind but gaining steadily. A couple of minutes later, the last of the shanties disappeared and they were running through open bush. The driver saw a puff of exhaust shoot up from behind the Toyota.

'Here they come!' he warned.

There was a bend ahead where the road disappeared into a dense clump of thorn bush. A fusillade of shots whipped past them. Now someone was standing up in the Toyota's open sun roof. He had a machine gun balanced on top. Was it Dinka? Sam could not be sure. A row of flashes raced towards the Land Rover. Sam fired back then ran out of ammunition. Grim faced, he realised he only had one full magazine left.

There was a loud bang underneath them. The Land Rover swayed and almost turned over. The air was full of the smell of burning rubber. A stream of sparks flashed past Sam's window.

'The tyres! They've shot the tyres,' the driver shouted.

Sam gripped the sides of the window and hung on. He could hear Kito screaming. The Land Rover was seesawing across the road like a dog with a broken leg and rapidly losing speed. He looked over the driver's shoulder and saw the bushes in front of them shaking violently and being tossed aside. He had a glimpse of shiny tank tracks, of radio aerials flexing. Then, an armoured car rumbled out of the scrub.

'Right! Let's go!' Captain Mbote ordered, and ducked down inside the Scorpion as it plunged through the thorn bushes. As they reached the road, he stood back up in the turret and checked both ways. Two vehicles were approaching from the same direction and moving very quickly. He was surprised. The road surface here was not good. There were ruts and potholes where last year's rains had washed away the tarmac surface.

'Wait!' he ordered, and stared at them through his binoculars. Something odd was happening. The first vehicle belonged to the UN. There was no mistaking the blue lettering on its side. And it was being fired at! No doubt about that either. He could see a man doing it. Who on earth would be shooting at a UN Land Rover?

The answer struck him forcibly. The rebels! Who else? He grabbed the intercom handset.

'Stand by, Gunner!' Then, 'Two vehicles coming up fast on your left. Your target is the black one. Black vehicle only. Got it?'

'Yes, sir. I see it! Black vehicle only.'

'One round . . . FIRE!'

The gun cracked. The Scorpion bounced on its tracks and the smell of cordite blew through the vehicle. The shell hit the road twenty metres in front of the Toyota. There was another loud bang and a cloud of debris shot up. A split second later, the Toyota appeared through the smoke with shattered windows and wobbling dangerously. The machine gunner was thrown out as the vehicle tried to turn. Smoke poured from its tyres. The brakes screeched and it rolled over and over in a cascade of glass and metal.

'Got him, sir!' the gunner cried, to much cheering from the rest of the crew.

There was a sudden whoosh as the petrol tank on the Toyota blew up. Scorching orange and red flames covered the wreckage of the large, black vehicle.

'Well, let's hope he really was one of Dada's lot,' Mbote said pensively. 'Better see how our UN friends are doing.'

He turned around and focused his binoculars. The

Land Rover was a hundred metres further down the road. Its front wheels were in a ditch. People were clambering out. Two men looking very shaken. He recognised Morrell at once. And two boys. Both armed. Child soldiers probably. They seemed to be all right. Mbote frowned and stared at them. He wondered. Was it possible Morrell had done what he had been asked to do? Could it just be . . . ? He fought to keep the emotion out of his voice as he bent down and called, 'Sergeant! Take a look back there, will you. Anyone you recognise?'

Sam flung out his arm towards the armoured car and danced a little jig. 'See, Kito? I told you they'd come.'

Kito stared at the trail of smoke drifting from the gun barrel. The UN man had been right after all!

'What's happened to Dada and the others?' he began to ask, when Sam suddenly gripped his arm.

'Look!'

A soldier was climbing out of the turret and jumping down on to the ground. A big man with three white stripes on his arm. Sam gulped. Now the man was running towards them. Waving. Calling.

Sam's gun slipped off his shoulder and clattered to the ground. He took a step forward. Unsure. Then,

'Dad! Dad!' he shouted at the top of his voice.

Kito watched them run towards each other with outstretched arms. He could hardly see. His eyes were streaming with tears. The big man bent and swung Sam off his feet and hugged him for what seemed an age.

Kito sank to the ground on his knees, then rolled over on to his side, and cried for his own father and the family he hardly remembered. He was inconsolable.

CHAPTER 38

'Have a drink, Patrick,' the President said, waving towards a well-stocked bar in the corner of his office. 'I think we deserve it, don't you?'

The Minister smiled and accepted happily. 'Not too much loss of life, I'm glad to say.'

The President laughed. 'Minimal. What you might call the bare essentials. Just Dada, his four-man escort and, I gather, some very nasty child called Binka. No! Dinka.'

He clinked ice into the glasses and opened a silver cocktail shaker.

'And meanwhile the diggings are running like clockwork.' He handed a glass to the Minister. 'Your brother-in-law, Mbote, did well, I hear. A neat surgical ending to what might have been a very messy operation.

Congratulations!' He toasted the Minister over the rim of his glass.

'It's playing well with the international press,' the Minister informed him. 'The British *Times* is reporting over a hundred children saved from a fate worse than death. And the *Washington Post* describes our actions as "courageous" and "an example to other African states".'

'Good!' said the President. 'Very good.'

Outside, the sun's rays were turning the room golden. The President went across and half drew a curtain.

'That boy, what's his name? Sam! He's back with his father? No problems there?'

The Minister shook his head. 'Cheerful little fellow. Lost most of his ear in a shoot-out. I liked him.'

'He's a lucky one, too,' said the President. 'He's got a father. Unlike the rest of them. Poor little brutes. Most of them are orphans. Their parents killed or scattered. No homes to go back to.'

'What do you want done with them? All these ex-child soldiers?'

The President stood up and began to pace up and down. The Minister recognised the signs and waited.

'I certainly don't want any of them here in Douceville,' he said, thoughtfully. 'We've enough problems with our own street kids without having this lot as well.' He peered out of the window, looking down at the busy street below. 'I'll tell you what my thinking is, Patrick. How does this sound?' He turned and faced the Minister.

'The diggings now belong to us. To the "people", I mean. And they look like being a great money earner. Just in time for the elections. However, we're still going to need an active and well-led security force, to stop greedy miners walking off with our,' he corrected himself, 'with the *people's* gold. Agreed?'

'Ye-es,' said the Minister, thoughtfully. 'And who will these guards be?'

'Patrick, you're going to like this.'

He went back behind his desk and sat down.

'I think,' said the President, 'that we should keep these child soldiers on as guards. With some positive changes, of course. We will give them smart new uniforms and better conditions. We might even pay them a little. Perhaps set up a school. Who knows.'

He looked at the Minister, assessing his reaction.

'I think we should call them "The Majungan Young Pioneers". Something like that. It sounds respectable. Noble even. We could give them Young Pioneer medals and awards, like a whole new branch of chivalry. Commander of Young Pioneers. Our generals would like it too, don't you think? Nice jobs in their retirement.'

The Minister looked dazed.

'Mr President,' he spluttered. 'These "Pioneers" of yours are just killers. Simple killers. Who would want to be in charge of them?'

'Well,' said the President confidingly, 'I think I can resolve that too.' His smile widened. 'In fact, I think I've got just the man for the job. They all know him. They respect him. He knows the ropes and seems to be in charge up there. His name is Simba. Calls himself "Colonel" Simba, I believe. I intend making his position official tomorrow, unless you have a problem with that?'

The Minister began to laugh.

'It's brilliant!' he spluttered. 'Congratulations, Mr President. It's brilliant.'

The President looked down at his desk top and gave a little sigh. 'Thank you. But if I'm totally honest, Patrick, it wasn't actually my idea.'

The Minister looked surprised. 'Not yours? Then whose was it?'

'Can't you guess? It was your old friend, Jack Schratte. Here! Have another drink. You seem to have spilled most of that!'

THE MAJUNGA HERALD

Established 1934

'Peace and Prosperity to our Nation.'

GOD'S FREEDOM ARMY SACKS VILLAGE

Eastern Province – Minister of the Interior, Patrick Mumba, announced today that crack units of the Majungan Army have carried out a highly successful 'Search and Destroy' mission and liquidated the leadership of the God's Freedom Army faction.

This evil rebel group, led by the self-styled 'Colonel' Dada, has been responsible for the deaths of thousands of people and the enslavement of countless children during its ten-year reign of terror.

It is reported that the attack on Dada's headquarters on the Baruba River was carried out by The Majungan Rifles. The Regiment reports the total destruction of Dada and his leading henchmen. There were no army casualties.

Our President, His Excellency Robert Nyuma, today paid tribute to the bravery of individual officers in the assault and thanked them for their dedication to the state. He also announced the setting up of a special mission to help recently liberated child soldiers adapt to normal life and conditions. This mission will, from now on, be known as the Majungan Young Pioneers.

His Excellency told the *Herald* that this initiative had received a warm endorsement from the government of the United States. 'It is a wonderful example for other African states to follow,' he said.

His Excellency also announced a preliminary meeting in Brussels next month with officials from a prominent Chinese-owned mining company.

POSTSCRIPT

Soon after his return to army barracks with his father, Sam spent two months at a UN sponsored Children's Rehabilitation Centre, in Bukavu. Here he received psychological recovery and social reintegration counselling which prepared him to re-adjust back into normal life.

While he still has nightmares and vivid mental flashbacks, he has coped very well. Sergeant Tembo took his son back to their village, Tshombe. The old headman, Francis MLindi, showed them the mass grave where Sam's mother and his sisters are buried. But Sam had the distinct feeling that he was not personally welcome there any more. Sadly, this is a common reaction on the part of many traumatised people to anyone who has been a child soldier in the past.

Sam has also been helped by having a father who is still alive and a safe, new home. He has found it much easier to return to normal life than Kito.

Kito is also being helped to re-adjust by the same centre that helped Sam. Right now, he is training to be a tailor although his stated ambition is to go on to college and become a teacher. His personal devils, however, are proving much harder to overcome. He suffers from long periods of depression and self-doubt. We wish him very well.

'Colonel' Simba's job title recently changed as a result of the Majungan government's new partnership deal with a Chinese gold mining company. He is now plain 'Mister Simba' but is the Manager of Human Resources at the old diggings. He also commands a detachment of the country's Young Pioneers. He is a popular member of staff.

Dinka, Colonel Dada and his escort all perished in the black Toyota. A couple of days after the incident, a gold miner poking around in the wreckage found three misshapen and badly burnt medals. Simba bought them off him for a half case of beer.

Jean Morrell has left the UN for a full time appointment as a mining consultant in Majunga.

Mr Schratte is alive and well and closely involved in the building of a new airport outside Douceville.

It will be called 'President Robert Nyuma International'. The President has a new ADC – a Major Joshua Mbote. He is rumoured to be 'going places'.

FACT SHEET

CHILD SOLDIERS

According to the latest UN statistics, there are approximately 250,000 boys and girls around the world, who are directly involved in armed conflicts. The charity War Child claims that girls make up forty per cent of this number.

While the great majority of these children live in Africa, child soldiers are unwilling combatants in countries as far apart as Burma (Myanmar) and Columbia, in Central America. In all, young people under the age of eighteen are actively engaged in wars or rebellions in twenty-four different countries across the globe. Most of them seem to be between the ages of nine and fifteen, although child soldiers as young as five, are not unheard of.

In the rural areas of Central and Eastern Africa, children have been kidnapped from their families for years. In the killing zones of eastern Congo and Rwanda, whole swathes of villages have been abandoned as families have fled to the towns in an attempt to protect their children. Until quite recently the same situation existed in many parts of West Africa such as Liberia and Sierra Leone.

Today, in the Democratic Republic of Congo and bordering countries, thousands of children are still being abducted at gun point. They begin a life of slavery, like the hero of this book, Sam Mbali.

Years of experience have given the war lords a devastating psychological weapon to use against normal, law-abiding people. These rebel militia leaders deliberately destroy the ties between the potential child soldier and his or her own society. One way of doing this, is to force the child to commit a violent public atrocity, often on a family member or a prominent villager. This makes it impossible for that child to ever return home. When the child has nowhere to go, the abductors become its new family.

Our own hero Sam Mbali was luckier than most. Even as he was led away, Sam knew his father was still alive and that as he was a government soldier, his father might be able to rescue him. This gave Sam a lifeline to cling to throughout his ordeal.

Child soldiers are not just used on the front line. They may also serve their masters as porters, labourers, cooks, spies and sometimes even as human shields. But whatever they are made to do, their lives are invariably short and brutal.

Why is there such a high demand for children?

Amnesty International reports that both government forces and rebel militias use children to fight their battles. Children are highly valued for a number of reasons:

- They are easily replaced. (Half the population of Africa is under eighteen.)
- They are easily manipulated because of their emotional immaturity.
- Once brainwashed, they are loyal and quick to obey and follow orders.
- They are more enthusiastic than adults.
- They do not need to be paid.
- Their stamina is often superior to adults.

Once the child soldier is trained to handle weapons, he or she is ready for combat. Immediately before the fighting begins, drugs are freely given to the children to start their adrenalin flowing. Crack cocaine and gunpowder, the so-called 'brown-brown', is the most popular combination. Its effect is well documented and turns children into fearless killers. In this story, Captain Simba refers to it admiringly, as 'Rocket Fuel'.

As if all this was not enough, many militia leaders also brainwash their children into believing that witchcraft and magic can protect them from enemy bullets. Our self styled Colonel Dada the Merciful, used to conduct full immersion baptisms before any major skirmish, claiming this 'magic' would turn bullets into water which would then run harmlessly off the children's bodies. And if the child was later killed or wounded, that was regarded as his own fault for not having sufficient faith in the magical powers of the Colonel.

For those child soldiers who do manage to escape, life is still difficult and very uncertain. People are terrified of child soldiers and have been for years. Their reputation for killing and destruction is known to everyone. Those who were victims of the militias, carry the scars. Returning child soldiers remind everyone of the massacres that took place, the burning of villages and the destruction of whole communities. No one wants them back. So the children drift into the towns and join the ranks of the homeless there. Rehabilitation centres are few and far between but they offer the only foreseeable hope for the future.

Pease is still a very long way off.

For further information, visit the following websites:

www.warchild.org.uk
www.savethechildren.org.uk
www.rescue-uk.org

AK-47 ASSAULT RIFLE

'Once you've fired an AK-47, you become brave.'

Sudanese Child Soldier, Emmanuel Jal

The Kalashnikov assault rifle (AK-47) was developed during the Second World War for use by the Russian Red Army. It has since proved to be the most successful rifle ever produced. Estimates of how many have been built since its first production in 1947 are believed to be in the region of 100 million – including all its different national variants.

It was designed for battlefield use and has a maximum effective range of three hundred metres. It has been used – and still is – in hundreds of conflicts and wars across the globe. It is extremely rugged and operates reliably in all conditions, from jungles to the desert. As it only has eight working parts, it is both cheap to produce and simple to use.

It has been described as a perfect weapon for child soldiers. It only takes an hour for an individual to learn how to fire and look after it. It is quite a heavy weapon weighing 4.3 kilograms without a loaded magazine. It fires 7.62mm bullets from a thirty round magazine. The bullets are designed to 'tumble' after striking their target. Which ensures maximum damage.